Murder

at the
Wimbledon Mansion

A Lady Marjorie Snellthorpe Mystery
Book 4

Dawn Brookes

Murder
at a
Wimbledon Mansion

A Lady Marjorie Snellthorpe Mystery

Dawn Brookes

Oakwood Publishing

Paperback Edition 2023
Paperback ISBN: 978-1-913065-76-8
Copyright © DAWN BROOKES 2023
Cover Images adapted from Adobe Stock Images:
Cover Design: John and Janet

Chapter 1

Lady Marjorie Snellthorpe had been questioning her decision-making skills since accepting an invitation to stay in Oscar Winchester's Wimbledon home. The man was virtually a stranger. Now, her car faced gleaming iron and decorated brass gates, framed by high, stately pillars of marble stone. A plaque on one of the pillars read Hallenguard Manor.

The gates slid apart as Marjorie's car approached, settling against their moorings with a gentle thud. Johnson, Marjorie's chauffeur, steered the vehicle through and onto the compacted stone driveway. Her eyes were drawn towards an enormous mansion visible through gaps in the trees.

Edna whistled. Marjorie could see why her cousin-in-law reacted as she did. The impressive Hallenguard Manor appeared and disappeared behind a row of elms lining the winding drive before finally being revealed in the distance, grand and proud.

Frederick shuffled in his seat.

"How do you know our host again?" he asked.

"I can't say I know him at all. Ralph and I knew his late father, Hugh Winchester, and his mother, Jasmin. It was a surprise to me when I received an invitation to stay with him. If I'm honest, he came across as a bit mysterious."

"I hate it when you say stuff like that, Marge," said Edna. "What's mysterious about being invited to stay with an old friend's son?"

"I'd find it odd as well," Frederick said. "I don't think any of my old friends' children would invite me to stay."

Marjorie was pleased when Edna opted for the least offensive response: an eye roll.

"It's peculiar because Oscar – that's Hugh and Jasmin's son – telephoned out of nowhere a few weeks ago, asking to speak to Ralph. After Ralph died, I got a few telephone calls from people who hadn't heard, but rarely these days. It took me a little while to remember who the man was, but as soon as he mentioned his father and how we had met once at a formal fundraising dinner, it all came back to me. The dinner was almost forty years ago, and from what I recall, Oscar was a rather petulant young man who enjoyed lording it over people. I didn't take to him, but we hardly spoke that night, so my feelings were immaterial.

"Oscar was studying at Oxford back then. My recollections are of him giving the impression he was a man's man. He drank too much brandy and spent most of the evening bragging to anyone who would listen about how good he was at everything. Ralph said he would grow out of it. The arrogance of youth, he called it."

Edna's head turned her way. "You still haven't explained what we're doing here or why you think it's mysterious."

"I'm coming to that."

"I know this driveway's long, Marge, but I don't think we've got all day."

Marjorie felt the usual irritation at Edna Parkinton's impatience. Six months had passed since the four friends had spent Christmas and the New Year together. Marjorie spoke to Frederick regularly, but to Edna less frequently, so it would take a little while to adapt once more to Edna's forthright manner. Nevertheless, Marjorie had grown fond of the woman, who had become a loyal friend, and she had mostly learned to ignore the brash side of her nature, as Edna meant no harm.

"When Oscar first telephoned, I had to break the news that Ralph was dead. He sounded upset – almost emotional – and went awfully quiet. It's not as if he knew Ralph that well. Anyway, there followed a rather awkward telephone call and I thought no more of it. I believe he mentioned he had settled in London – his parents travelled a lot, you see. I must have told him about our upcoming visit to watch the tennis at Wimbledon because a few days later, he called again and said we must come and stay with him."

Horace had phoned her a fortnight before Oscar's impromptu call to offer Marjorie, Frederick and Edna the use of his company's debenture tickets for the second week of the tennis tournament. The tickets had become available when one of his sons decided to meet clients in Australia rather than in the UK. Marjorie always watched the British Grand Slam when she could and had been delighted, as had Frederick when she asked him if he was available. Edna had been less enthusiastic, but hadn't wanted to miss out, so agreed to come.

"Let me get this straight. Out of the blue, this Oscar bloke, who you haven't seen since he was barely out of nappies, invites you and your mates to stay with him for a week?" Edna said.

"Yes, that about sums it up, apart from him barely being out of nappies, but I take your point: when we met, he was a young man. He told me he and his wife would be staying at their Wimbledon home throughout the summer and that they also had debentures. He was quite insistent. I assumed when I explained there would be four of us, it would put him off, but he said his house was big enough for all of us to stay. His trump card was saying he would like to offer us hospitality out of respect for Ralph and his late father. I tried once more to tell him it was kind of him, but we wouldn't want to impose. Despite my reluctance, he was rather pushy. In the end, I gave in. It is, after all, so much closer to the tournament than my home is and saves us having to meet Horace inside the gates every day. I'm afraid that's when I accepted on our behalf. I suppose it's not that mysterious, but I explained all this to Horace."

"Well, Horace didn't explain it all to me." Marjorie watched Edna shooting Horace a stern glare. "He just told me our plans had changed, and we'd be staying closer to the tournament. Until he met me at the train station this morning, I thought we'd be in some expensive hotel, all bills paid and all."

"It's good of the chap to invite us along, and convenient for me as it turns out," said Horace. "I'd forgotten the grandkids planned to stay in my London flat this week. It was nice to see them, but also noisy, if you know what I mean. We spent the weekend together, and I took them to the theatre and whatnot, but I think they were overjoyed to see me go. I was cramping their style."

Johnson stopped the car next to a black limousine with privacy windows.

"Blimey!" exclaimed Edna, stepping out first. "I think I'm going to enjoy staying here. This place makes you look poor, Marge. Good job you brought the Rolls, or they'd send you away."

Edna was right about the extravagance of the house and the grounds which, from what Marjorie could see, were immaculately kept. The perfumed scent of flowers greeted them, along with the smell of freshly cut grass, and a plethora of birdsong rang out from the trees. Dappled sunlight provided some welcome shade as Marjorie climbed out of the car.

Edna was marching around, gawping at the impressive building.

Oh dear. I hope I've done the right thing bringing her here, thought Marjorie, before admonishing herself for being such a snob. She reminded herself once more that she and Edna had become much closer during the Christmas break than she had ever imagined they could, and she'd like to build on that rather than tear it down.

Frederick was the last to get out of the car and appeared reluctant to move any further. Horace hummed while he took his and Edna's suitcases from Johnson while Edna marched towards the steps leading to towering black doors.

"Are you going to be all right?" Marjorie asked Frederick.

"Sorry. I don't feel comfortable with all this." He nodded towards a couple of men dressed in white uniforms who were standing in Horace's way. Johnson was following with an extra bag. "I suppose that's why you kept it from me until last night."

"I am sorry about that." Marjorie had feared Frederick would back out if she told him in advance about the change of plans, having been looking forward to his company. "They are just people, Frederick. Wealth and titles don't make a person. It's what's in here." She put her hand to her heart.

Frederick attempted a smile. "I'm sure you're right, but I'm out of my comfort zone staying in places like this. I tend to say the wrong thing."

"If it's any consolation, we'll hardly be here. I intend to spend most of the time watching tennis. Consider it bed and breakfast," she said, grinning. "A rather grand bed and breakfast, I grant you."

Frederick gulped, his mouth a thin line as he forced a smile. "I'll try." The furrows across his forehead deepened. "I'll get our suitcases. It seems Edna's collared your chauffeur to follow those men dressed in white."

Sure enough, the two dour men had taken Horace and Edna's suitcases and the extra bag, and Edna was pushing Johnson to follow them. One of the men was exceptionally tall and the other short and stocky.

Marjorie sighed. "Surely she doesn't think they're going to steal her underwear!"

Frederick guffawed, retrieving their luggage from the back of the car. His grey eyes danced in the sunlight. He really was rather handsome when he laughed. It was good to see him again, but before Marjorie could go into a teenage tizzy, one of the men in white returned and wrestled their suitcases out of Frederick's hands without uttering a word.

Frederick smirked. "I say, did you see that? Perhaps Edna has a point."

Johnson returned to Marjorie, somewhat frazzled. "I'm sorry, Lady Marjorie, but—"

"Don't worry, Johnson. We saw what happened."

"I'll wait in the car while you get settled, then," he said.

"I'll see if someone can bring you refreshments. We shouldn't be long," Marjorie replied.

At home, Johnson would have waltzed into her kitchen and helped himself to tea, but she wasn't sure how formal Oscar would be about employees. She hadn't expected men in uniforms or such a large and imposing mansion.

Marjorie and Frederick exchanged glances as they walked up the steps to the opened black doors. The mansion was a grand piece of architecture from another era, with its tall windows, gables and stonework decor. Manicured Virginia creeper grew up the walls and around the doors and windows of the front facade. Marjorie felt a thrill of anticipation as she studied the entranceway – it really was magnificent. Yet clearly Frederick was feeling apprehensive; he had furrowed his brows again and his hands twitched nervously at his sides.

Marjorie's pleasure turned to anxiety as she felt her heart thudding against her chest. She looked at him, silently urging him to remain composed. Everything would seem better once they were inside.

The men in white had dumped their luggage in a large hallway and came outside to hurry them along. Frederick had no choice but to keep walking. Once they entered, the two men closed the doors behind them with a resounding bang.

Chapter 2

The taller of the men in white spoke for the first time. "Wait here."

There was no sign of their host when Marjorie and Frederick gazed around the expansive hallway with its sparkling black-and-white marble floor tiles. The room was filled with marble columns and chandeliers as far as the eye could see. A faint smell of lavender drifted through the air.

Edna couldn't resist wandering around, her heels clopping on the tiled floor while she perused paintings, ornate vases and sculptures set on top of pedestals.

"Would you look at these?"

"Don't!" a voice thundered, but it was too late. Edna was already in motion, clutching a heavy sculpture which she almost dropped.

An overweight but muscular giant with ice-cold brown eyes and short-cropped fair hair snatched the statuette from Edna and returned it to its place. He glowered at Edna before addressing Marjorie.

"This way please, Lady Marjorie."

"How did he know you were the lady and not me?"

Marjorie suppressed a giggle as she and the rest of the party followed the domineering man, keeping their distance.

"Please leave things alone," she hissed at Edna.

"I only—"

"Marjorie's right," said Horace. "We don't know how valuable things are, Edna. Best not to drop a family heirloom and offend our host. At least not until we've settled in."

Edna's painted lips protruded into a pout. Her usually bright expression had given way to a sombre one. She lowered her eyes to the ground, drooping her shoulders slightly. She could ignore Marjorie's rebukes, but not Horace's. It was good to have him along. He was the only one Edna listened to, and also, he liked her, so she took his remarks as intended, whereas Marjorie could never quite get her criticisms right.

"Do you suppose he's a butler of some sort?" asked Frederick.

"He might be, but he looks more like a brawny bodyguard to me, almost as wide as he is tall. Did you notice the hooked nose? I'd say it's been broken at least once."

Frederick chuckled. "I was too busy looking at the size of his hands. They're like meat cleavers."

"He's also carrying a weapon," said Marjorie.

"What kind of weapon? I didn't see a weapon," Edna complained.

"A gun. It's holstered beneath his jacket." Marjorie tapped the left side of her ribs to show where she had seen it. She resisted the temptation to point out that her cousin-in-law had been too busy meddling with priceless antiquities to have noticed anything.

"He can't do that. It's illegal," whispered Frederick.

"Perhaps it's a replica," she said.

"Still illegal," muttered Frederick. "And Edna might have been wrong to pick up the statue thing, but he had no right to growl at her like that. Who does he think he is?"

"Yeah, see. I'm glad Fred's on my side."

"That's not quite what he was saying," Marjorie muttered to herself.

The group continued to follow the colossal figure ahead of them until they reached a set of ornately carved double doors made of ebony. Once they caught up with him, Marjorie heard raised voices coming from the room on the other side. Their guide's square jaw set even harder before he raised a fist to knock. Marjorie saw one of the hands Frederick had been referring to and had to agree it was gargantuan. The giant wore a gold sovereign ring on the third finger of his right hand.

The door flew open and a slight woman with tanned skin and long black hair that flew behind her like a scarf stormed past without so much as a glance in their direction. The only hint of her passing was the scent she left in her wake. Marjorie vaguely recognised the man glaring after her.

Oscar Winchester was forty years older and shorter than she remembered, but the extra weight he carried made him a more formidable presence than when they had first met. Despite the passing years, though, he had the same arrogant look.

Edna's eyes were on stalks, still following the woman's retreat, and Horace's jaw had dropped. Frederick was behind Marjorie, but she imagined his reaction would be similar. Oscar, noticing them, pasted on a smile and strolled towards her with arm outstretched.

"Lady Marjorie! Welcome to my home. It's so good to see you again after all these years." He shook her hand effusively while kissing her on both cheeks, which she felt was overcompensating for what they had just witnessed.

She and her friends walked into a lavishly decorated room with plush carpets, velvet curtains, and paintings adorning each wall. Oscar's smile was friendly enough, but his blue eyes were hard.

"And these must be your friends."

Horace was the first to recover, putting his hand out. "Horace Tyler. Thank you for having us."

Oscar took the hand and shook it before turning away. "And you must be an angel from heaven," he said, looking at Edna, who was wearing her favourite red wig. His greeting was playful, with a teasing glint in his eye.

Edna shot Marjorie a smirk as she replied. "Pleased to meet you, Mr Winchester. I'm Edna. Edna Parkinton."

"Oscar, please. We don't do formality here. I trust we'll be friends, Edna." He gave her a suggestive wink.

"I'm sure we will," said Edna, grinning through the heavily plastered makeup.

"And this is Frederick," said Marjorie.

"Pleased to meet you," said Frederick shyly, not sounding pleased at all.

While the two men shook hands, Edna shot Horace an 'I've still got it' look. Horace's eyes wrinkled with mirth.

"Do come in, Jamie," Oscar clicked his fingers. "Why didn't you tell me our guests were here?"

"I was on my way to do so, sir."

So much for 'we don't do formality here, thought Marjorie. "We've only just arrived. Jamie here was kindly showing us the way."

Jamie straightened. "Should I leave you to it, sir?"

Although the words were subservient, the tone was not. Marjorie suspected Jamie didn't like his boss very much, and from what she had witnessed so far, she couldn't blame him.

"Have the car ready in forty minutes."

"Right."

"Are you sure you don't mind us imposing on your hospitality, Oscar?" Marjorie asked, hoping for a last-minute reprieve.

"I can assure you, it's no imposition. You are most welcome."

"Then could I ask another favour? Johnson, my chauffeur, is outside. I wonder if he might have a cold drink?"

"Of course... Jamie!" Oscar bellowed after the fast retreating man. "Show Lady Marjorie's chauffeur to the kitchen and get someone to give him a drink and some food."

"Yes, sir," Jamie snarled back through gritted teeth.

"Don't mind him. He's the most miserable man I've ever met, but he's a damn good bodyguard."

"I didn't think it was legal for bodyguards to carry weapons in this country," said Frederick.

Oscar scowled. "What? He's not carrying that thing again, is he? The gun's licensed, but he's supposed to keep it under lock and key. Jamie likes to push the boundaries." Oscar gave a false laugh.

"Is he ex-military?" Horace asked.

"No, worse. He's an ex-heavyweight boxer, more brawn than brain, but he likes to think he's Arnold Schwarzenegger. Don't you worry about the gun; I'll have a word. Now, make yourselves at home. I hope you'll like my humble abode…"

Edna spluttered as Oscar continued.

"…This is my sitting room. I'll introduce you to my wife later."

"Was that your wife leaving just now?" Horace asked.

"Oh, her. No. That was Paris, Paris Toliver. She owns a London escort company and is a friend of the family. She stays here sometimes. I've got some other people staying and I've just informed her of a change of plans for today. You might have noticed she wasn't happy about it."

Understatement, thought Marjorie.

Oscar shrugged. "Paris overreacts."

Marjorie had hoped that time and the recent loss of Oscar's father, which she'd read about in *The Times* obituary, might have matured him from the young man she had met all those years ago, but it appeared not. When she had told him about Ralph's death, he had sounded genuinely sympathetic, but alas, this was the same egotistic person of forty years ago, just older. Now he had the status, power and wealth with which to lord it over people. She should never have agreed to accepting his hospitality and now she had put her friends in a difficult situation.

Thank heaven for the tennis.

The men in white who had wrestled their luggage from Johnson and then dropped it off in the hall appeared, carrying a loaded tray.

"Please take a seat," Oscar motioned to some chairs, and a sofa upholstered in dark red leather. The men laid the tray on an elegant mahogany table in the centre of the room and poured tea and coffee from solid silver pots. Marjorie appreciated tea from a pot, and owned a small silver one herself, although she used a china teapot these days. Horace and Edna opted for strong coffee while Frederick joined her in accepting a cup of tea.

Once the men left, Oscar played the perfect host, lavishing praise on her and being attentive to her friends. Whilst Marjorie enjoyed the perfectly brewed tea, she was counting the minutes until they could make excuses and leave without being impolite.

Horace, as always, appeared at ease and chatted to Oscar about their respective businesses. Oscar had inherited a worldwide hotel chain from his father; Horace's firm specialised in avionic components. The latter had done business with people all around the world and was a good match for Oscar, who, it turned out, also had an interest in aircraft engines. The conversation flowed easily between them; it quickly became clear that they shared a certain level of ambition, despite their very different backgrounds.

Marjorie was proud of Horace and admired his ability to be at ease in any company. Frederick was the complete opposite. He was uncomfortable, looked out of place and barely said a word. Marjorie attempted to draw Frederick into the conversation, but with little success. Instead, his gaze constantly shifted between the teacups and the cake dishes on the table before him.

In between eyeing the extravagant sitting room and its contents, Edna chipped in on the men's conversation with quips that made them laugh. Oscar was positively flirting with Marjorie's cousin-in-law, but Marjorie could tell by the way he kept looking at Edna with a sly smirk on his face that he was playacting. This situation was deteriorating rapidly.

Marjorie could feel an underlying tension in the room, and she hated how Oscar's wealth was intimidating Frederick. She was more convinced than ever that her friend would find it difficult to stay in such an exotic mansion, and she feared that Oscar's arrogance and Horace's confidence were only making things worse.

Marjorie had a feeling there was an ulterior motive behind Oscar's hospitality. She needed to find out what it was.

Chapter 3

Marjorie was about to ask if they could be shown to their rooms when a glamorous-looking woman entered. She was taller than Oscar and statuesque. Blonde hair cascaded down to her shoulders and a sleeveless pink summer dress hugged her curves. She wore a beautiful ornate gold bracelet and a heavy matching necklace. High-heeled sandals added to her height and grace.

Marjorie noticed her flawless skin shining under the light. She had to be twenty years younger than Oscar. The smooth floral fragrance of Oud Ispahan, a Christian Dior perfume, replaced the musky scent left behind by Paris Toliver.

Oscar stood and pulled the woman close to him, placing a heavy arm around her waist. "Allow me to introduce you to my gorgeous wife, Georgina. Darling, this is Lady Marjorie Snellthorpe, who I told you about." A veiled warning in his tone alarmed Marjorie, but the others didn't seem to notice. Georgina's beauty bedazzled the men, and Edna was fawning over the carat weight of the gold.

Georgina pulled away from her husband. "Delighted to meet you." She extended a hand towards Marjorie. The hand was tremulous. Her lips curled upwards in a forced smile, which barely reached her dark eyes.

"And I you," said Marjorie, smiling warmly. She assumed this was an unhappy, perhaps convenient, marriage, on the wife's part at least.

Oscar next introduced Horace, Frederick and Edna, who all still appeared unaware of the underlying tension. While Oscar resumed his technical conversation with Horace, Georgina stepped into her role as hostess, hiding her original uneasiness.

"You have a beautiful home," said Marjorie.

"Thank you. Do take a walk around the grounds when you have the time. The gardens are exquisite."

Marjorie got the impression Georgina was speaking by rote, and she couldn't help noticing the occasional glances between husband and wife. She wondered if there were any children. Neither had mentioned any, and Marjorie would not pry.

"I'd love to know more about the history of this place," said Frederick. "I can imagine the Victorians holding some incredible balls here."

"Hugh would have been the one to ask about that. Oscar isn't interested in history." Georgina checked Oscar wasn't listening before adding, "I prefer our home in Cannes."

Marjorie nudged Edna to get her to close her mouth. Oscar and Horace finished their technical conversation and rejoined them. Georgina seemed relieved.

"I'm sure our guests would like to see their rooms before they leave for the tennis, Oscar. And I need to get myself ready," she said with a smile.

"Thank you," said Marjorie. "That would be most kind."

"Our plans have changed, sweetheart. We're going to watch tennis today. I've just told Paris to cancel the royal tour." Oscar's lips were taut and his eyes hard.

Georgina reached for her cheek as if he had slapped it. "You told me you were working today. Paris promised me a tour of Buckingham Palace. Then I was going into Knightsbridge to do some shopping."

Oscar batted away her arguments with a wave of his hand. "It's all taken care of. Paris will show us the Centre Court instead and the shops will still be there another day.

We'll join you for dinner, Lady Marjorie. I hope you don't mind?"

"Of course not," said Marjorie, minding very much indeed, not quite believing his nerve. "We shall look forward to it."

Edna's eyes bulged, and a frown crossed her face. She muttered to Horace, "What a cheek."

Georgina opened her mouth to speak again, but Oscar interrupted. "Not now, darling. As you say, our guests need to unpack." Ignoring the scowl from his wife, he summoned one of the men in white who was hovering in the doorway.

"Before you go, Lady Marjorie." Oscar took Marjorie's arm and guided her towards the window. "I apologise, but I'm sure you've guessed I have another reason for inviting you here. I would have spoken to your husband, but… well… anyway."

"What is it you need?" Marjorie asked.

Oscar lowered his voice. "We'll talk tonight. After dinner. I need your advice on something and it's imperative you keep this conversation, and what I tell you, a secret, even from my mother." Then his voice got louder. "We'll look forward to dining with you later, Lady Marjorie," he said before nodding to the man in white.

Marjorie and Edna exchanged a look as they followed the man, who had been joined by his equally surly companion, back along the corridor to the main hallway and up a wide spiral staircase with marble steps. The deep red walls rose towards a domed ceiling, while intricate carvings adorned each of the balustrades. The gleaming mahogany handrail, though worn by a century of use, looked as elegant as it must have done when it was new. Edna's heels echoed with every step.

"I'm not sure Frederick liked the idea of Oscar joining us for dinner," Marjorie said.

"Your face wasn't the picture of joy either, although no-one else would have noticed. Bloomin' gall of the man."

Marjorie chuckled. "I must work on my facial expressions."

"And what was that little side conversation all about?"

"I have no idea, but I'm delighted to hear his mother is still alive. Why didn't he mention that on the phone? I'd have been much happier about staying if I'd known."

"You're rambling, Marge."

"It's rude of Oscar not to have told me dear Jasmin would be here. Now I'll have to wait to catch up with her in the morning."

"But what was he saying? Is his mother ill?"

"I don't think so. He said he wants to talk to me later. It sounds like he might be in a spot of bother, but who knows? He might want to ask for an introduction to someone Ralph knew. It's kind of him to host us for the week, but I can't warm to him at all."

"He's rich and arrogant, that's all. I wonder what the place in Cannes is like. Maybe we'll get an invitation for a winter jolly. I hate British winters."

"I do hope not," said Marjorie.

"Anyway, Marge. Whatever his trouble is, I wouldn't mind this sort of bother." Edna chortled as she waved her hand to incorporate the surroundings, but then had to stop to catch her breath.

"Are you all right?" Marjorie asked.

"I'm not good with stairs these days, and these blokes are in a hurry. Look at them go."

Edna looked pale. Marjorie hoped she wasn't unwell.

The men carrying their suitcases had raced up the stairs. One of them was hurrying along the wide internal balcony overlooking the hallway. The stockier man was walking at a more leisurely pace, but still faster than Marjorie and Edna were used to. Horace and Frederick had paused on the landing, having a whispered conversation. Marjorie was grateful to Horace for trying to put Frederick at ease.

When Edna and Marjorie caught up with the tall man, he stopped and pushed open a large door, placing Edna's case down outside while indicating to Marjorie that she should enter with a nod of his head. Without a word, he stepped by her and put her suitcase down.

"I guess this is me. Thank you," Marjorie said to the man, but he was already heading next door, with Edna shuffling after him.

"And this must be me," Edna shot back over her shoulder. The taller man retreated quickly and Marjorie watched as the older and not quite so fit man showed Horace to the still vacant room next to hers and Frederick to the one on the other side of Edna. Marjorie felt relieved they were all close together and stepped into her room.

It was more like a suite than a bedroom, with massive high ceilings and a Queen-sized bed against the wall, in the centre. She wouldn't have been surprised had it been a four-poster, but the furniture and soft furnishings were all modern. There was a chaise longue and an ornate padded chair along with a large dressing table. The ensuite bathroom housed a bathtub and sink served by ornate gold-coloured taps and trappings. A separate shower with a gold-coloured shower head was behind the door and a WC and bidet, also adorned with gold handles and buttons, completed the facilities.

Returning to the bedroom, Marjorie was dismayed she hadn't had the opportunity to say anything else to her friends before they were shunted into their rooms, but grateful she wouldn't have to worry about bumping into either of the men in white if she was caught short during the night. A display of freshly cut summer flowers in a vase on the dressing table made her feel more at home. It's what she would do when guests stayed in her home.

Marjorie unpacked her suitcase with mixed feelings. The decision to stay with Oscar may not have been a wise one, but she felt happier knowing her old friend Jasmin was somewhere in the house. Nevertheless, she should have checked with her friends before accepting the invitation, and now Oscar was being presumptuous, crashing in on their evening. Marjorie had little concern about Horace settling in and making the best of things, but she feared Frederick would be tense, which, as he had admitted, didn't bring out the best in him. Edna was likely to clash with the austere Jamie, although she seemed to get on well with Oscar, whose dismissal of the bodyguard's handgun did not convince Marjorie he would deal with the situation. She was also slightly worried about Oscar's behaviour towards his wife.

It had been the memories of a long-ago friendship with Hugh and Jasmin that had clouded her judgement, along with the faint hope that Oscar might have mellowed. He had been so friendly on the phone. The atmosphere downstairs and the way he had behaved with Paris Toliver, Edna and Georgina made her feel uncomfortable.

Marjorie was hanging the last outfit inside the generously apportioned wardrobe when she heard a bash at the door. Without waiting for her to reply, Edna burst

in, closing the door behind her, breath chugging like a
steam train.

Chapter 4

"Whatever's the matter?" Marjorie asked.

"This ain't what I expected, Marge. I don't care how rich this guy is, or how big his place is, I don't fancy being in a house where blokes like that Jamie fella and, for all we know, the men in white are tooled up. I've a good mind to ring the police. And speaking of Jamie, I wouldn't trust him with a water pistol."

Edna's outburst brought on a coughing spasm. Marjorie waited for her to get her breath back.

"Have you quite finished?" Similar thoughts had crossed her own mind, but Marjorie wouldn't have quite put them like Edna had. She wondered if Edna's tirade had more to do with Jamie snapping at her about the statuette incident than his carrying a gun.

"You can't fool me, Marge, that's not your sort of thing either."

"Quite right. I can assure you I didn't know there would be guns on the premises. But Oscar promised us he'd see to it the gun gets locked away. I wonder if the rules are different in one's own home. If it makes you feel better, I regret accepting Oscar's invitation, but we're here now, so we'll have to make the best of it. Have you asked Horace what he thinks?"

"Didn't get the chance. Every time I poke my head out of my room, one of them men-in-white guys is loitering. There's one out there now, probably listening through the keyhole." Edna folded her arms.

"Don't be absurd!" Marjorie said, while moving further into the room as a precaution.

Edna lowered her voice. "Horace ain't answering his mobile, either. He's probably taking a shower or something. Anyway, I've texted him and told him we need to talk. I don't like it, Marge. Maybe your mate Oscar's worried about a threat from one of his own people."

Marjorie couldn't help thinking Edna might be on to something. Jamie, for one, gave the impression he didn't like his boss, although he seemed to do as he was told.

"If it is something like that, all will be revealed this evening."

"Did you see how Oscar's wife shook when he touched her?" Edna went on.

"I didn't think you'd noticed. You appeared quite at ease while he was flirting with you," Marjorie said.

"That was before I met the man's poor wife, and before I had time to think. The woman's obviously upset about his changing her plans and he enjoyed telling her, if you ask me. Not to mention that Paris woman flying out of the room like she was being chased by a herd of elephants. The man's a megalomaniac. If I were Paris, I'd fly back to my office and not return."

Edna paused, taking a seat on the chaise longue in Marjorie's room while catching her breath. She rubbed her hands along the smooth velvet upholstery.

"This is nice. I've just got a chair in mine. Nothing like this."

Marjorie was more concerned about Edna's health than the room furnishings, hoping the breathlessness wasn't a return of the cancer Edna had previously received treatment for. The treatment that had left her with alopecia, hence the many wigs.

"I see you found the time to change your hair," she said, smiling.

Edna adjusted the blonde bob until it fell in a soft wave across her face. "Do you like it? It's a new one. Some women buy shoes, I buy hair."

"The short style suits you," Marjorie said, relieved that it wasn't the beehive Edna had turned up wearing at Christmas. She didn't mention the potent scent of the hairspray might not be helping with the breathing difficulties. Instead, Marjorie returned to the subject of Oscar. "It's such a shame he isn't more like his father. Hugh was a gentleman in every sense of the word."

"Is Oscar an only child?"

"Yes. Jasmin suffered terribly in childbirth, rather like myself, and decided not to have any more children."

"You never told me about any suffering. I just assumed you wanted to stop at one."

"It's hardly something one discusses over lunch," said Marjorie, fighting back the awful memories of when she'd nearly died after giving birth.

"I suppose you're right. At least you've got Jeremy, although your friend might have been better off without an Oscar."

"That's a terrible thing to say, Edna, even for you."

Ignoring the rebuke, Edna continued. "And while we're discussing Oscar – not that I'm endorsing Jamie here, but Oscar treats him more like a servant than a bodyguard."

Marjorie sighed. "Let's try not to be too hasty to judge, Edna. We've only been here a few minutes. It's quite possible that we've caught them at a bad time. We've witnessed a few moments of friction for which there might be an innocent explanation. It shouldn't lead us to unfavourable conclusions too prematurely. I agree with you Jamie needs to put the gun away, and I hope Oscar keeps his word and tells him to lock it up. Other than that, it's a run-of-the-mill elite household."

Edna snorted. "If you say so, Marge. You believe that if you want to."

"I take it you were being facetious when suggesting the men in white could be armed?"

"Maybe, but anything's possible. They look like the knife-carrying types to me. For all we know, they could have a hidden arsenal. You might not have noticed the dangerous-looking swords and knives sheathed in belts all around the place. There's enough weaponry hanging on the wall in the hall to start a mini war. What these people are doing here is against the law. You need to make it clear to Oscar we will not stand for any lawbreaking."

"You're exaggerating, but I suppose I deserved that. It's I who got us into this situation, and I abhor weapons of any kind, no matter whose hands they're in. I believe the weapons downstairs – which I did notice – are of the ornamental variety." Marjorie would have had to have been blind not to see the sabres and paraphernalia on the walls downstairs when they followed Jamie to meet Oscar. "However, I will have a word with Oscar as you suggest and ensure Jamie has put his weapon where it belongs. We can discuss any other concerns with Horace and Frederick when we're out. If they're not comfortable staying here, we can leave after I've seen Jasmin. It might be embarrassing, but I'm past the time of life where that matters. It's not as if we're prisoners."

"Not yet," Edna huffed. "I wouldn't put money on it staying that way. What if we're held hostage?"

"For what purpose? Don't entertain such thoughts, Edna. This is England," said Marjorie, firmly. "You're letting your fears get the better of you again. Remember, I knew this man's father and I hope to see his mother. Out of respect for them, I ask you to treat Oscar Winchester cordially, and do nothing to offend him."

"Don't you worry about me; I'll play the game. Anyway, he likes me. But I can tell you now, him and Jamie give me the creeps. We should leave at the earliest opportunity. Your Fred doesn't look at ease…"

Marjorie frowned.

"…don't look at me like that, Marge. You know you like him – though what you see in him, I'll never know."

"He's not rude for one thing," Marjorie muttered under her breath. "Let's discuss this elsewhere." Marjorie was worried about Edna's rising voice and her suggestion there might be someone listening at the door. "Why don't we get out of here and watch some tennis? I believe lunch awaits us in the debenture restaurant – I expect there will be a glass of champagne to go with it, which should steady our nerves."

Edna grinned for the first time. "Now you're talking, Marge. I'm not into tennis, but I'm very much into champagne. You'll need to watch it don't go to your head, mind. You're not as young as you used to be."

Marjorie picked up her handbag. "One is as young as one feels, and at the moment, I'm feeling well enough to cope with a glass of champagne. Thank you." The reality was, Marjorie was feeling anxious and full of regret, but there was no use giving in to such feelings or making Edna's nerves any worse.

"We're going to need all the sustenance we can get if we're going to survive a night in this place."

"You really have changed hymns. On the way upstairs, you said you wouldn't mind these sorts of problems."

"Yeah, but I don't own the place. If I did, that lot would be out on their ear."

Edna didn't say which lot she meant, but Marjorie assumed she was referring to Jamie and the men in white.

"Let's go." Edna crossed the room and yanked the door open wide. When Marjorie followed, she half expected to catch one of the men in white with an ear to the keyhole, but instead was pleased to see Horace coming out of his room. He put a finger to his lips.

Heeding it as a warning, Marjorie checked over her shoulder to see one of the men in white hovering close by. Perhaps Edna had a point, but why should they be interested in her party? The logical explanation was that they had been told to be on hand in case any of them needed anything. If they didn't look so menacing, Edna wouldn't be entertaining the fantasy that they had some sort of malicious intent. Instead, she'd be flirting.

"Where's Fred?" Edna asked.

"He knocked to tell me he'd be waiting for us downstairs," said Horace.

It didn't surprise Marjorie to hear that Frederick was in a hurry to leave. She would listen to what Oscar had to tell her over dinner, but felt sure they would be packing their bags and leaving once she had seen Jasmin the following morning.

"I'll just be a moment," she said, returning to her room. Once inside, she inhaled and exhaled slow, deep breaths, trying to dispel the uncomfortable sensations from her mind and body. She then retrieved the small jewellery box from the bedside drawer and placed it inside her handbag. One couldn't be too careful. She also checked the door to make sure it had a lock and was pleased to see a key, which she also placed in her handbag. She was certain there would be a master, but if she left hers in the lock while she slept, that would at least keep anyone from entering uninvited.

You're getting as paranoid as Edna, she chastised herself.

Chapter 5

Edna shared her fears with Horace and Frederick on the journey to the All England Tennis Club. Horace tried to reassure her, explaining he had met many wealthy businessmen over the years and that whilst Oscar was brusque with those around him, there was nothing nefarious going on in the Winchester household.

"But what about the way his wife shook?" Edna asked.

"She seemed more angry than frightened to me," said Horace. "I expect she didn't want to make a scene in front of guests. Believe me, Oscar would have got a right earful once we were out of the room."

"Trust you to stick up for the man," Edna moaned.

"I'd be the first to intervene if I saw any sign of mistreatment, Edna, so don't say such things."

"Horace might be right. I saw Georgina while I was waiting in the hallway. She was sparkly, laughing and joking with someone on the phone," Frederick said.

Horace rested a hand on Edna's. "It will become obvious soon enough, and if there's anything untoward going on, we'll leave. But remember, some men – and women – are more authoritarian than others."

Edna folded her arms. "What about Jamie and his gun?"

"Agreed. That is odd," Horace conceded.

"Not to mention illegal," said Frederick.

"And the knives? I suppose the knives are just part of the dress code?" Edna wasn't giving up so easily.

"The men weren't carrying knives, Edna, that was your assumption," said Marjorie.

"And perhaps Oscar's spoken to Jamie by now. I don't mind checking with him later," said Frederick.

"For someone so timid, you've got real backbone sometimes," said Edna, almost admiringly.

"In the meantime," Frederick continued, flushing slightly, "we should try to enjoy the man's hospitality out of respect for Oscar's father and Marjorie's late husband."

"Oscar's mother, Jasmin, is in the house somewhere. I find that reassuring," said Marjorie.

Reluctantly, Edna nodded. "As long as Johnson is on standby in case we need a rapid exit," she said.

"Would that be all right with you, Johnson?" Marjorie asked.

"It's all sorted. Mr Winchester came down to the kitchen and suggested I stay on the third floor with his staff to save me driving from north to south London to take you backwards and forwards to the tennis. I accepted. I hope you don't mind, Lady Marjorie."

"I had thought we would get taxis, but it will save us the bother," Marjorie said. She would have preferred Johnson to be offsite, but couldn't interfere now arrangements had been made.

"That's settled, then," said Horace.

Johnson dropped them off at the entrance and went to park the car. He told Marjorie he'd go home to pack a bag and would queue for a ground ticket later on, or wait in the car if he got bored or light stopped play. She agreed to call him once they were finished for the day.

After a lengthy three-course lunch, which took longer to digest than Marjorie had hoped, the only drama taking place that afternoon was played out on the tennis court. All the same, Marjorie couldn't help sneaking the occasional peek over her shoulder to check there were no strange men nearby. She couldn't shake the troubling feeling that their movements were being watched. It was irrational. Edna's neurosis was becoming contagious.

They saw two women's singles and one men's singles before the match they were watching came to an abrupt end. A player slipped at the back of the court and, after receiving treatment for an injured knee, only managed another two games before retiring.

"Now might be a good time to go to dinner," said Horace.

Marjorie asked what the time was.

"Time you wore a bloomin' watch," said Edna.

Marjorie sighed. "I suppose I asked for that."

"It's six-thirty," said Frederick. "I could do with some food myself. I've only had a couple of glasses of Pimm's, but the alcohol's gone to my head."

"I told you not to drink it like cordial," Edna chastised. "You should also put some sun cream on your head. You're lit up like a lightbulb!"

Marjorie had to concede that Frederick was looking sunburnt. It wasn't like him not to wear a hat to protect his bald head.

"I forgot my hat when rushing to get ready," he said.

Marjorie felt guilty. Frederick had been uncomfortable for the whole time they were at Oscar's house.

"There are plenty of caps for sale. You should buy one," suggested Edna.

Marjorie was reluctant to move. She would be happy to go for dinner if it weren't for her unease about meeting

Oscar – and most likely Jamie – in the debenture restaurant.

"What's the matter, Marge? Ain't you hungry?"

"Nothing's the matter. I'm enjoying the tennis and want to make the most of being here." The next two players had walked onto the court and were warming up. "I almost wish we had brought a picnic."

Horace leaned over, whispering, "Don't fret, Marjorie. Edna told me Oscar wanted to speak to you. Best to get it over with."

"What are you two on about? Get what over with?" Edna snapped.

"Dinner," said Marjorie, feeling suddenly queasy. Horace was far more astute than she gave him credit for, whilst Edna had drunk far too much champagne.

"Oh. I know what you mean now. You don't want to see Oscar and his harem."

"Edna!" Marjorie checked around. Thankfully, the booth was empty apart from the four of them.

"No harm meant."

"Please be a little more circumspect. We don't know who might be listening."

"Marjorie's right, you know," said Frederick. "I keep feeling we're being watched."

"Is this the same man who said it was okay to stay with an armed gang out of respect for Ralph Snellthorpe?" Edna mocked.

"I'm serious. I've been thinking…"

Edna rolled her eyes.

"…There was something odd going on this morning and I can't get it off my mind. I suggest we pack our belongings and leave first thing tomorrow. I've got a friend who owns a house not too far away from here. They're out of the country most of the year. I'll make a call after dinner. We might even go tonight." Frederick's eyes pleaded with Marjorie's.

Edna opened and closed her mouth, but decided against whatever it was she was going to say.

"If none of you are happy staying, I have no objections, although I think you're overreacting," said Horace.

"Please do that, Frederick. I must say, I'm not looking forward to returning to the mansion myself, but I would like to speak to Jasmin before we leave. Tomorrow would be my preference. I have fond memories of Jasmin." Marjorie didn't mention that Jasmin was also one of the few people still alive who had known Ralph.

"Brilliant plan. Now let's eat," said Edna, heading out of the booth and racing like a greyhound, as if her life depended on her getting to the restaurant before anyone else. A few people muttered and tutted as she barged past them.

"I don't think our Edna is a tennis fan," said Horace, grinning.

"Then I suppose we must be thankful to her for making the effort to come," said Marjorie.

The trio walked towards the restaurant at a more leisurely pace. Marjorie's stomach churned, feeling like she was an animal about to be slaughtered. This wasn't like her. She wasn't prone to bouts of paranoia. That was Edna's role. It was time to shake off the cloud that had hung over her and her friends for most of the day.

She inhaled deeply, bracing herself to tell Oscar they wouldn't be staying for the entire week after all. Even if Frederick's friend couldn't put them up, they would find a hotel or she would ask Johnson to drive them back and forth from Hampstead for the rest of the tournament. It was only an hour's drive from her home on the outskirts of London. They could even take the underground.

"I'll break the news to Oscar over dinner," she said to Frederick.

Except she couldn't tell their host anything over dinner because Oscar wasn't there. Neither was any of his entourage. Although relieved in so many ways not to have to suffer an atmosphere while dining, Marjorie was annoyed at his rudeness, for both demanding to join them and not having the decency to turn up, and she was disappointed. She would, of course, attempt to see Jasmin before leaving tomorrow, but she would have to tell Oscar about their change of plans when they got back.

Frederick was obviously irritated too. He looked glum and picked at his food.

"See," said Horace, "I'm an excellent judge of character. The wife got her own way, after all. My bet is Oscar's not as scary as he makes out."

"Maybe you're right; perhaps we're worrying over nothing," said Frederick.

Somehow, Horace's theory made them all feel more at ease. Horace and Edna were cheery, eating four-course meals while chatting away, although Edna ordered Horace not to discuss tennis.

"It's enough watching a ball go side to side over a net without analysing it afterwards," she said. "At the end of the day, it's just a game."

"That's like saying cricket is just a game," said Horace.

Edna scowled, then giggled. "It is. Although if I had to choose, I'd go for tennis rather than cricket."

"I can't believe I'm asking, but why?"

"Because the men wear shorts in tennis," Edna replied, snorting with laughter.

"If I'd said something like that about women wearing short skirts, you'd say I was sexist."

"Yeah, well. You should know by now you can't win."

Horace grinned and complied with Edna's request, keeping any thoughts about the tennis to himself. Marjorie and Frederick, however, discussed the matches they had watched. It turned out they both loved the game and could analyse some of the better shots and game plans.

By the time dinner was over, Edna had drunk even more champagne, making Marjorie fear what she might say next. She needn't have worried. Edna fell asleep after finishing the large dessert.

Horace grinned. "Perhaps we should call it a day. I doubt the last match will finish tonight, anyway. Even if they close the roof, there's an 11pm deadline."

Horace was right. Marjorie had kept an eye on the scores via the screen in the restaurant and it was already 9.30 and one set all.

"I suppose it would be polite not to arrive back at our host's too late on the first night. You'd better wake Edna. I'll call Johnson once we're leaving the grounds." Although Johnson had said nothing, she was sure he'd agreed to stay at Hallenguard for her sake. He was as loyal to her as he had been to her late husband, and he was nobody's fool. He would have sensed the atmosphere in the Winchester household. And if he'd had any doubts, their conversation on the drive to the tennis would have put paid to them.

"I'll try to call Hazel from the car. It was too noisy in there," said Frederick.

"Hazel?" Horace raised an eyebrow.

"My friend Hazel."

"Ooh, get you! Don't tell Edna, or she'll be talking about you and your harem," Horace teased.

"I didn't say my friend was a man, did I?" Frederick was almost crowing. "Actually, she's a doctor who trained with my wife. We still meet up from time to time."

By the time they'd roused Edna and given her the amount of black coffee she demanded, and her condition required, another hour had passed and people were flocking from the grounds. Marjorie was pleased she had decided to leave calling Johnson until they actually left the club or he'd have been worried.

"I see you've got yer phone with yer for a change," Edna slurred.

"Not only that, it's a new one, I notice," Horace teased.

"Jeremy insisted on replacing my old one when he found out the battery was no longer charging. I don't know why I didn't have one of these before. It's much easier to use than my last one. I can even send emails and go on the internet. I have a shopping app and all sorts of things, not to mention I can now listen to audiobooks when my eyes are tired."

Edna's eyes rolled. Marjorie wasn't sure whether it was because of the amount of alcohol she had imbibed or from sarcasm.

"Thank the Lord for your son. Welcome to the twenty-first century, Marge." The comment left Marjorie in no doubt it had been the latter.

"I've got the same make," said Frederick. "Have you tried video calling yet?"

"Jeremy keeps trying to call me on what's something or other, but I can't seem to work out how to answer with the video on, and then he gets cross because I hang up."

"You have to unlock the screen," said Horace.

Marjorie was half-listening as she dialled Johnson, but the phone was snatched from her hand before she had the chance to say anything.

"Let me show you, Marge… Hello? Who's that? Oh, Johnson, it's you. Yep, we're on our way, we're just coming through the gates. See you in a few minutes."

Edna insisted on trying to show Marjorie how to use the messaging app to make a video call while staggering along with the tennis crowds piling through the gates towards the carpark.

"Look, Edna. This isn't the time. Show me later. Now please give me back my phone before you drop it."

Edna pouted but did as requested. Horace took her arm when she almost fell into a hedge.

"Let me be your guide," he said.

Marjorie sighed.

Chapter 6

By the time they had left the grounds it was half-past eleven, and almost midnight when Johnson pulled the car up in front of Hallenguard Manor. Two other cars were parked in the driveway, but the limousine from the morning wasn't.

"Looks like Oscar and company are still out," said Horace.

"Oh dear," said Marjorie. "I was hoping not to have to see the men in white without their boss in residence."

"Serves themselves right."

All heads turned towards Edna, who had been snoring most of the way home. She opened her eyes and rubbed them.

"Serves who right?" Horace asked.

"What are you talking about?"

"Never mind," said Marjorie. "You were dreaming. We've arrived at Oscar's, but the limousine isn't here, so it looks as though we won't be able to let him know we'll be leaving in the morning."

"Good. I'm tired," said Edna.

"You can be obtuse at times," remarked Marjorie.

"Why?"

"Thirty minutes ago, you couldn't wait to tell Oscar what to do with himself," Frederick reminded her.

"That was before you phoned your friend and she said she'd rented her place to a group of tennis players," Edna retorted.

"So you weren't asleep for the entire journey, then," said Marjorie with a twinkle in her eyes, unable to resist teasing her cousin-in-law.

"Asleep? I was just resting my eyes, but I heard everything that's been going on. Anyway, I'm sure it won't be that bad staying with Oscar for the week. At least it's free."

Frederick's mouth drooped.

"We'll talk about it again in the morning once I've spoken to Jasmin," said Marjorie, patting his upper arm.

"So, why are we sitting here? I need some sleep," said Edna.

"I suppose we should get out and ring the bell?" Horace shrugged.

Johnson took a shiny key from his breast pocket. "I've got a key for the staff entrance, if you wouldn't mind going in that way?"

"Oh, that sounds far more exciting," Marjorie answered. "And preferable to meeting the men in white. Lead the way, Johnson."

The quartet followed Marjorie's chauffeur around the side of the house and down three steps to a shiny black door.

"This is one of those mansions they could rent out to film producers," said Horace.

"Oscar doesn't strike me as a man who would want actors swanning around his home," said Edna.

They followed Johnson along a corridor leading to an enormous kitchen. The lights were on, but nobody appeared to be around. Marjorie scanned the room. The kitchen was Victorian in feel, but had been completely restored and fitted out with all the modern appliances and accessories. The range was brand new and heated the room much like hers did at home.

"I say." Horace whistled.

"Makes your place look like a shack, Marge."

Marjorie grinned. Edna was recognising that although Marjorie lived well, it was all about the scale.

"In which case, ours would look like matchboxes," said Frederick, sighing.

"Let's see if we can sneak upstairs and get to bed," suggested Marjorie.

"Not before I've had a nightcap," said Edna, smoothing out the blonde wig which had taken up a leaning tower position.

"I can't see how we can do that without rummaging through cupboards, for which we don't have permission." Marjorie wondered if she was missing something; she couldn't see any drinks laid out. "Besides, you've had enough for one day."

Edna frowned. "There were drinks on a sideboard in that lounge where we met Oscar earlier."

Trust you to notice, thought Marjorie.

"Marjorie's right, Edna. It's time to call it a night unless you want to risk bumping into your friend Jamie on your travels." Horace steadied Edna as she walked into a chair.

Marjorie gave Johnson a nod. "I assume you know the way?"

"It's through here." Johnson opened a door and stood back. "There's a set of stairs at the end of the corridor leading up to the main hall. Would you like me to check the coast is clear?"

No sooner had Johnson finished speaking than they heard men's voices heading in their direction. Horace shrugged.

"Looks like we're busted."

The men in white from earlier were now dressed in grey. They stopped talking when they saw Marjorie and friends. Edna spluttered, suppressing a giggle.

"What are you doing down here?" It was the taller man who snapped the question. He had a stern, angular face and a prominent jawline. His straight black beard was neatly trimmed.

"We've just arrived back and didn't want to disturb anyone, so Johnson brought us through this way. If you'll excuse us, gentlemen, we've had rather a long day and would like to retire for the night." Marjorie stepped forward, expecting one of the men to stand aside and let them pass.

They barred the way.

The shorter and stockier of the two held Marjorie's gaze with penetrating sky-blue eyes, a mirror image of her own, but far colder. She noticed a large mole over his left cheekbone and tried not to stare.

"Mrs Winchester has waited up for you. Please follow me." He about-turned and marched back the way he'd come. The four reluctantly followed him while Johnson distracted the other man by asking him where he could get a cup of cocoa.

"At least they're not Jamie," whispered Frederick.

Marjorie let out a sigh of relief. "We have to be thankful for small things. I wonder where Oscar has got to if Georgina isn't with him?"

"I wouldn't mind having a chat with Georgina before going upstairs—" Horace let out a yelp when Edna elbowed him in the ribs.

"Don't start with yer flirting, Horace Tyler. Remember, Oscar's bodyguard has a gun."

"Has there ever been a man more misunderstood?" Horace winked at Marjorie.

The man in grey, whose name they still didn't know, turned left when they reached the door to Oscar's sitting room. After leading them along another small corridor, he stopped at the end to knock on a door before opening it.

The group inside ceased talking when the man announced the arrival of Marjorie and her friends like something from a historical novel. However, it wasn't Georgina who stepped forward. She wasn't there... it was Jasmin, wearing a beautiful purple silk evening dress. Her bright green eyes lit up.

"Marjorie! How wonderful to see you! When Oscar told me you were coming to stay, I was thrilled."

"The pleasure's all mine," said Marjorie, accepting the warm embrace from the woman who was around the same age as herself. She again wondered why Oscar hadn't mentioned his mother during their telephone conversations. "May I introduce you to my friends?"

Edna's gait was still a little unsteady when she stepped forward. Horace kept a supportive hand on her arm while shaking Jasmin's.

"What an honour it is to meet any of Lady Marjorie's friends," he said.

Marjorie remembered Jasmin had held the title of Lady Jasmin Michaels before her marriage, but dropped its use at her late husband's request. Hugh was a self-made businessman, much like Horace, who loved his wife deeply but never wanted to be part of what he called the entitled set. Despite his opinions, he and Ralph had got on well, and Ralph respected him for his achievements and their shared philanthropic interests.

Following the introductions, Jasmin moved her eyes back to the others in the room who had resumed their own conversations. She took Marjorie's arm.

"I'd love to catch up with you and have a long chat later."

"I'd like that," said Marjorie, wishing it could have kept until the next morning. Late nights didn't suit her.

"We can disappear as soon as Oscar's home. I was hoping they would be back by now."

"Where is he?" Marjorie asked. "We were expecting to meet him for dinner. He told us he, Georgina and Paris would be at the tennis."

"Yeah. He wanted a word with our Marge here," said Edna.

Jasmin's eyes widened. "Oh? What about?"

"He didn't say, did he, Marge?"

Jasmin studied Edna.

"Edna's Ralph's cousin… from Burnley." Marjorie hoped that would be enough to explain Edna's bullishness, but she didn't know whether she felt more guilty about her generalisation of the population of Burnley or pigeonholing her cousin-in-law, who was unique.

Jasmin smiled in Edna's direction, but Horace was frogmarching her towards a couple of men smoking cigars by an open window in the corner of the room.

"Usually people pussyfoot around as though I'm made of glass. I like her frankness."

"Edna's an acquired taste, but she's turned out to be a good friend."

Jasmin raised an eyebrow. "I never had you down as a snob, Marjorie."

"Neither did I until I met Edna. Unconscious bias, I think they call it these days. Although there's more to our differences than mere etiquette."

"But you've got through them."

"It's a work in progress," Marjorie replied. "You never said where Oscar was?"

"Paris took him and Georgie to Buckingham Palace. I don't know why he'd say he was going to the tennis. He hates it."

Marjorie was puzzled. "Doesn't he have debenture tickets?"

"They were Hugh's. My husband went to the tournament every summer for as long as I can remember." A faraway look appeared in Jasmin's eyes before her voice dropped and could barely be heard. "I miss him so much. It's like—"

"I know what you mean," said Marjorie. "There are few people our age to share the memories with, and even fewer who knew Ralph."

"What about your friends?"

"Edna's more of a recent widow than I. She misses her husband, but when we talk family... well, it's complicated."

"I remember now. Wasn't it her father who was disinherited in favour of Ralph?"

"Precisely. So we get on better when we avoid those sorts of conversations. Horace is a widower, but wasn't close to his late wife. He was a bit of a playboy in his youth, but he's a lovely man."

"And the fish out of water... Frederick, did you say?"

"How observant you are. Frederick's a retired pharmacist. His wife was a doctor, he's a widower and misses her. None of us knew each other's spouses, except for Edna and I. Somehow when I'm with the three of them, I'm able to forget about the past. They have become my present."

"I have someone like that. David Cribb is the closest friend I have." Jasmin pointed to a smartly dressed man in his early eighties who was chatting easily with Frederick. "David was Hugh's most loyal adviser and friend."

Marjorie saw the sparkle return to Jasmin's eyes. Perhaps David was more than a friend.

Loud guffaws drew their attention to the opposite corner. Edna was where she liked to be: centre of attention. The two men she and Horace had joined were laughing while she told them an entertaining story, no doubt from her days as a singer.

"Are those men Oscar's friends?" Marjorie asked. They both looked to be in their late fifties. One was smartly dressed, wearing a designer suit. He was tall with dyed black hair. The other was medium height, rounder with fair hair and a bushy beard and moustache. His shirt was unbuttoned at the neck, but he wore a loud orange tie.

"Terence, or rather, Terry Kemble and Gordon Collins. Terry – the taller of the two – is one of Oscar's oldest friends and mostly runs the European side of our business.

Gordon is the family accountant. I've met him a few times at social gatherings, but don't know him well. It was his father Hugh and I knew. Mason Collins retired recently and handed over the reins to his son. If it wasn't for ill health, I think Mason would have worked until he dropped. Alas, he's in a nursing home following a stroke. Gordon is competent enough and Oscar seems to like him."

Marjorie wondered why the accountant would be at a private gathering, but didn't like to pry.

As if reading her thoughts, Jasmin said, "He's not here as a guest. He arrived earlier this evening insisting it was important he speak to Oscar." Jasmin opened her palms. "I didn't feel I could send him away, so invited him for dinner. He wouldn't say what it was he needed to see Oscar about, but reassured me it was nothing that should worry me. My son's not the best money manager. I expect he's forgotten to file or sign something important."

Marjorie sighed, thoughts turning to her own son, Jeremy. Widows and their extravagant sons; it appeared she and Jasmin had a lot more in common than she had imagined.

"I'm so sorry we lost touch," she said.

"Me too. But what was to be done? Hugh and I spent so much time abroad it was difficult to keep up with old friends. Hugh spoke to Ralph a few times a year. I always asked after you, but you know what men can be like when they're talking business."

Marjorie chuckled. "Indeed I do."

Without warning, Jasmin teetered to one side. David Cribb and Frederick moved just in time to catch hold of her. They helped her to a large settee, where Marjorie sat on one side of her and David Cribb on the other. His forehead creased, light blue eyes frantic.

"I told you it would be too much for you. Oscar should be here. It's not right. I'm going to call an end to this."

"Don't." Jasmin grabbed his forearm. "It's nothing, David. I've been standing for too long, that's all."

"Why don't you go to bed?" Marjorie suggested. "We can talk in the morning."

"I apologise for being rude. I'm David," he said to Marjorie.

"Marjorie," she returned.

"Marjorie's right," he said, turning back to Jasmin. "Frederick and I can escort you to your room. I'll come back and stick around to make sure this lot are okay before I go to bed."

"Perhaps I will call it a night, if you don't mind. Would you join me for breakfast in my room, Marjorie?"

"It would be my pleasure," said Marjorie. "I'll come with you now so that I know where to find you."

Chapter 7

Jasmin's suite at the rear of the mansion was like a small apartment. The wallpaper was a serene lavender, and the walls were adorned with signed watercolours. A large mantelpiece was the centrepiece of the sitting room, and tall bookshelves lined the other walls.

There was enough light for them to see by coming from an illuminated conservatory at one end. Marjorie noticed an easel set up with a half-painted portrait, but it would be impossible to make out whose portrait it might be without crossing the room. In view of her friend feeling unwell, she didn't want to appear rude.

"Do come in," Jasmin instructed the three of them. "This is where I spend most of my time when we're not entertaining."

"Should we remove our shoes?" Marjorie asked, not wanting to damage the plush cream carpet.

"You don't need to," Jasmin said.

The two men helped her into a deep-backed sofa. David, who was taller and in better shape than Frederick, did most of the supporting. He flicked the switch on a standard lamp. The sweet scent of fresh summer flowers from a vase in the centre of a mahogany coffee table drifted through the room.

"Shall I get you a brandy?" David asked.

"I'd rather have a mug of hot chocolate if that's not too much trouble."

David clearly knew his way around Jasmin's personal quarters, switching on other standard lamps and turning off the light in the conservatory before heading straight through a door off to the left, which Marjorie presumed led to a kitchen or kitchenette. She could hear the ticking of an antique clock with pendulum swinging, which stood in the centre of the mantelpiece.

"Are you sure you don't need a doctor?" she asked Jasmin.

"Heavens, no! I'm just a little overtired, that's all. I'll have a tonic once I've had the chocolate."

"You should have let me deal with the guests." David reappeared, placing a mug of hot chocolate on a coaster on the table in front of Jasmin.

"You worry about me too much, David." Jasmin's voice was tender.

"Frederick and I will leave you to rest, Jasmin. I look forward to seeing you in the morning," said Marjorie. "I hope you have a good night's sleep."

"I should say that to you, Marjorie. After all, you're our guest."

"Well, goodnight, dear," said Marjorie.

"Goodnight, Marjorie. And thank you, Frederick, for helping."

"My pleasure," said Frederick.

Marjorie and Frederick retraced their steps, walking along corridors and reaching the main hall leading to the spiral staircase.

"I'll see you to your room," said Frederick.

Marjorie felt she should protest, but there was something reassuring about being escorted back to her room in a strange house.

"Thank you," she agreed.

"Jasmin seems nice," said Frederick.

"Yes, she's one of those people who sees nothing bad in the world. But I got the impression she's worried about something." Marjorie had been mulling over the conversation she and Jasmin had before the unfortunate funny turn.

"Did she say what it was?"

"No. In fact, she didn't admit to being worried in so many words. I hope to find out in the morning. It will mean I won't be joining you and the others for breakfast, though."

A flicker of concern crossed Frederick's face, but he said nothing. There was nothing else she could say to reassure him, so she tried a different subject.

"What do you think about Oscar leaving his mother to entertain his guests while he swans off to Buckingham Palace for the day?"

"The same as I thought about the Christmas fiasco." Frederick's temple pulsated and his face flushed when he realised what he'd said. "Sorry. That was tactless."

"Don't be. I won't criticise my son in public, but you're quite right. He left us in a pickle, didn't he?"

"David Cribb seems very fond of your friend." Frederick's voice sounded whimsical. Marjorie knew that sometimes he wanted a closer friendship with her than she was prepared to give, but she appreciated the change of subject.

"I thought the same thing. She says he was Hugh's oldest friend and an advisor. I suppose that's why he looks out for her."

"I like him, although he seemed to fuss over her. He's got an air of sincerity about him. At least he'll protect her from her son."

Marjorie didn't wish to revisit the subject of selfish sons, so they walked silently along the landing until they reached her room. "Would you say goodnight to Edna and Horace when you go back down? Tell them I've done my share of socialising tonight."

"So have I. I'll nip down and tell them what happened in case they didn't notice, and then go to bed myself. Goodnight, Marjorie. Sleep well."

"At least the men in white… now grey… aren't loitering tonight."

"I expect they're partying with Johnson in the kitchen while the boss's out. You know what they say about cats and mice."

Marjorie grinned at the image. "They don't strike me as the partying types. Goodnight, Frederick." She entered her room, retrieving the key from her handbag and closing and locking the door behind her.

***

Some hours later, Marjorie heard car doors slamming and voices breaking through the still night. She had left her window open, feeling the need for fresh air. As soon as it was quiet once more, she drifted back to sleep.

Marjorie woke again a short while afterwards. The pillows were a little too firm for her liking and were giving her a stiff neck. The soft hoots of an owl in search of its prey played out in the distance, along with the chirping of crickets. A breeze had got up and blew welcome air through the humid room. She heard leaves on the trees outside the house rustling in the wind.

Sleep eluded her after the second awakening because, when she had reached out for a glass of water to quench her thirst, there wasn't one. Thirst always seemed a lot worse when there wasn't water to hand, she mused. Marjorie rose and sat on the edge of the bed, listening to the wind and other night sounds. The owl had gone quiet.

After sitting for a short time, she decided it was no use, her thirst needed to be assuaged. She switched on the bedside lamp and tiptoed to the en suite, not knowing whether the floorboards were the old, creaky kind. Discovering one particularly loud one, she stepped over it.

There wasn't an empty glass in the bathroom and she opted not to use the beaker where she had placed her toothbrush, unsure how clean it would be. There was nothing to it but to get dressed and risk an expedition to the kitchen. At least she knew where it was.

Thankful that her new phone had a working torch, which her previous one hadn't, she used it to guide her way downstairs, carrying her shoes in one hand and the phone in the other. All was quiet when she crossed the dark hall, glancing from side to side before putting her shoes on and venturing down the stairs she and her friends had climbed earlier when following the man in grey.

"I really must find out his name, and that of the tall one," she muttered.

Once inside the spacious kitchen, Marjorie felt it was safe to switch on a light, finding the switch just where it should be. "One thing about the Victorians, they had a sense of order. Some houses these days have light switches in the oddest of places." Marjorie found speaking out loud made her feel better about wandering around someone else's home in the dead of night.

She opened and closed a few of the dark oak cupboards until she found one packed with an assortment of glasses. After filling a large tumbler with tap water, Marjorie took a hearty drink. The tap water had a slight metallic taste, but it was refreshing enough to moisten her mouth and throat. Rather than refilling the glass from the tap, she checked the fridge and found bottles of mineral water. She refilled the glass from a small bottle and tasted it.

"Much better," she said.

The kitchen was stifling hot because of the range, so she would be happy to leave. Just as she got to the door leading into the passage, she heard a noise behind her. Feeling a sudden chill of fear run down her spine, she whirled around, her heart racing, pounding in her chest, only to see a large ginger tomcat casually munching on food from a bowl near the sink.

Instinctively, she clutched her chest, trying to quell the fear that had bubbled up inside her. "You almost gave me a heart attack," she muttered. The ginger tom stopped eating for a moment, staring at her with his emerald eyes. Then he meowed. There was something comforting about the company of a feline which Marjorie couldn't explain.

Cats are such intelligent creatures.

"What's your name, then?" Marjorie asked while the cat purred and rubbed against her ankles, having finished his meal. She leant down to stroke his thick, soft fur, upon which he purred louder. Stroking the cat was calming after the fright he'd given her a few moments before.

Marjorie reached for his name tag. "Sorry, I'll never be able to read that without my reading glasses. Let's call you Mr Tom for now. Time to say goodnight, Mr Tom." She smiled at the literary reference as she switched off the light and used her torch again. The cat followed her along the passageway, turning right at the foot of the stairs.

"I see. This is where we go our separate ways. Goodnight, puss."

Marjorie paused when she heard the cat meowing and scratching at something. Sighing, she placed her glass down on the step while she went to see what the problem was. He was scratching at a door.

"Hmm, Mr Tom," she said. "Someone's shut you out of your bedroom, have they?" Marjorie turned the handle, which creaked loudly. "Are you sure this is your room?" she asked the cat. The door was stiff. It took all her strength to push it open, slowly scraping against the floor tiles. She almost jumped out of her skin when a flash of black passed through her legs.

She stared after the demented animal, recovering and giggling nervously. "Any more friends you would like to tell me about, Mr Tom?" The ginger cat meowed, waiting patiently for her to push the door wider. It suddenly gave way past the resistance and Marjorie almost fell inside.

The room was black with no window, so she shone her torch on the wall to find what she was looking for and flicked the light switch. The sight that greeted her made Marjorie's stomach lurch. A gasp of horror escaped her lips. The loud pattering of paws on floorboards was only eclipsed by Mr Tom's yowls as he fled.

Chapter 8

A Victorian laundry hanger was suspended from the ceiling, high above Marjorie. Gordon Collins dangled beneath it with a rope tied tight around his neck. The man's eyes were bulging and unseeing, his mouth was open as if he'd been taken by surprise by the force of the drop. His head was tilted unnaturally to one side and his suit was creased and dishevelled, although the orange tie was still in place. The body was limp and lifeless.

Marjorie stared at the thick length of rope, partly to keep her from looking at the poor man any longer than necessary. It wasn't from the hanger and she thought it strange he hadn't used that rope. His shoes had fallen or been kicked to the floor. A four-legged stool lay on its side. Presumably, Gordon himself had kicked it away. The smell of death hung in the silent air.

Marjorie shook herself from a trance and into action, retrieving her phone from the floor where she had dropped it beneath the hanging man. Luckily, it wasn't broken. She made an emergency call, requesting an ambulance and the police.

The operator put her through to ambulance control, who then put her through to the police. The desk sergeant told her not to touch anything, but she knew better than to do so anyway.

Marjorie moved back towards the door, almost tripping over Mr Tom. "Oh, you've come back, have you? Where were you when I needed you, Scaredy-cat?"

The ginger tom gave her a disgusted and disapproving look, then left. "Don't blame me, I didn't put it there." Mr Tom meowed from the passageway as if it was her fault the corpse was still in his bedroom.

Marjorie pressed the speed dial on her phone. It was answered immediately.

"Hello, Marjorie. I take it you can't sleep either?" Horace sounded wide awake.

"Not now, I can't. One of the men you were drinking with this evening is sleeping permanently. I'm in the scullery where Gordon Collins, the accountant, is hanging."

"Suicide?"

"That's what it looks like."

"I'll be right down. Where is it?"

"Take the stairs down as if you're going to the kitchen, but turn left at the bottom, and then it's the first right. I'll wait for you in the passage."

Horace appeared almost as soon as she ended the call. He was dressed, but in a different suit from the one he'd worn the day before.

"I couldn't sleep," he explained. "After taking a shower and changing, I've been sitting in the chair all night just in case you ladies had any trouble with... well, you know..."

"The men in grey."

"Where is he?"

Marjorie motioned towards the open door with a movement of her head. Horace stepped inside, but stayed close to the door so as not to tamper with the evidence.

"Poor fellow."

"What kind of rope is that?" Marjorie asked.

"The one around his neck, you mean?"

"Yes. It doesn't seem to belong in the room."

"Hmm. It looks like hemp rope to me. If someone enjoys climbing, sailing or fishing, it's common enough. It's made a big comeback in recent years, being environmentally friendly and waterproof."

"But why would it be in here?"

"Perhaps he brought it with him. Maybe, for some unknown reason, he wanted to make a statement by killing himself in Oscar's home." Horace rubbed his chin, frowning at the sight in front of him. "Shame we can't let the pitiful man down from there."

"Quite, but I was told to leave everything as it is." It didn't sit comfortably with Marjorie either, but she didn't want to risk the wrath of the police. "How did he seem to you last night?"

"Happy enough, although I got the impression something was troubling him."

"That's at least three people, then," said Marjorie.

"I'm not sure I'm following."

"Don't mind me. The cogs are working overtime. I mean, that's three people who appear to be worried in this household. Oscar, Jasmin and the dead man. Jasmin said he had urgent business with Oscar, but nothing to trouble her with. Did he say anything that might have hinted at what was on his mind?"

"Nothing. Mind you, Edna and Terry were doing most of the talking."

"And he didn't hint why he was there?"

"No. At first, I assumed he was staying, but when we said we were going to call it a night, he knocked back his drink and said he was leaving. We hung about waiting for Terry, but Edna was getting tired. Terry Kemble's in a room along our corridor. I was still talking to Edna on the landing when he passed us, so he definitely went to bed."

"When Jasmin told me Gordon was Oscar's accountant and needed to talk to him, she implied Oscar wasn't efficient at handling the financial side of the business."

"That's nothing unusual if his company's as big as it sounds. You can't keep your hand on everything. Terry seems to manage quite a lot for Oscar from what I heard him telling Edna, but other than that, we talked about Europe. Terry spends most of his time in France. I asked Gordon what he did for a living, of course, but other than saying he was an accountant, he said no more on the subject. To be fair, company finance is not the most riveting party conversation.

"Oscar and Georgina were still out when we went up to bed. I heard them come home about an hour or so later. Gordon could have hung about downstairs longer than he said he was going to – no pun intended. It's a big house. He could have gone into Oscar's sitting room and waited until the house was quiet to do the deed."

"What about the men in grey? Did you see anything of them?"

Horace shook his head. "I assumed they had retired for the night. The only other thing I saw was when I took a sneak peek out of the window when the others came back. Georgina stormed into the house, leaving Jamie and Oscar having a bit of a barney, from what I could see. They were quiet about it, but the body language suggested an argument. Especially when Oscar poked the guy in the chest. Laughable really… one punch from Jamie and he'd be flat on his back."

Marjorie chuckled. "I'd have liked to have seen that. I heard car doors banging as well, but didn't look out. Was the unhappy escort, Paris, not with them?"

"No, didn't I say? Just after Fred told us you and Jasmin had gone to bed, she made an appearance. Fred left just before she arrived. She told us she'd come back with a headache after eating out with the others, but was feeling better. She's staying in the house at the moment as well. It seems guests are always stopping off here, and she looks after them. Oscar and Georgina had gone on to a nightclub."

"When they have guests staying?"

"That's what I thought. David Cribb was back in the room by then, and he wasn't impressed. He and Paris left together. I think they went for a private chat, because I saw light coming from under the door of Oscar's sitting room when I went to use the facilities. It wasn't on when we went to bed."

"What time is it now?"

"It's 4.30am. It tells you on your phone, you know?"

"Of course it does. Shall we go upstairs so the paramedics don't wake the household?"

"Good idea," said Horace. "We can't do any good here, anyway."

Marjorie pulled the scullery door to where the resistance prevented it from being fully closed and followed Horace up the stairs to the main hall. He was always good in a crisis.

"What were you doing down there, anyway?" Horace asked.

"I needed a glass of water." Marjorie let out a heavy sigh, realising she hadn't brought the replenished glass up with her. The scratchy throat would have to survive. At least she'd had one glass before finding the body in the scullery.

No sooner had they arrived at the front door than a paramedic's car pulled up outside. A woman hurried up to where they were waiting, leaving a driver in the car.

"What happened?" she asked.

"Follow me," said Horace. "You wait here, Marjorie. I can show this lady where the body is."

It wasn't long before the paramedic and Horace arrived back.

"I'm told you found the man," she said to Marjorie. "When was that?"

"A few moments before I called you and the police. They said they would also send an ambulance."

"Which is just coming up the drive now. I'm a first responder and was closer. Hang on a minute, I'll let them know I've confirmed death."

"You weren't long down there. What did she do?" Marjorie asked Horace.

"Well, it's pretty obvious the man is dead, but she donned overshoes, climbed on the table and checked his neck for signs of life. She couldn't reach to listen to his heart with her stethoscope without falling off the table and she wasn't happy to move him without the say so of the coppers, just in case."

Marjorie watched as the three paramedics spoke in hushed tones, gesturing and nodding to each other in a quiet confab. The glint of the ambulance's blue light illuminated them and their green coats flickered with colour in the pre-sunrise gloom.

"You would have thought the police would be here by now, wouldn't you? I'd like to break the news to Jasmin before they arrive."

"I don't mind waiting here if you want to go on. There's nothing else we can do until they decide what they want to do. I'll make sure no-one else uses the stairs until the police get here. Do you think we should wake the others?"

Marjorie shook her head. "Let them sleep. Edna will have a terrible hangover and Frederick... well... he's likely to be upset. They'll find out soon enough."

Leaving Horace to man the front door, Marjorie tiptoed along the corridor towards the back of the house, dreading the task ahead. Jasmin Winchester was unwell. That had been made obvious by her funny turn and David Cribb's reaction to it. How was she going to break the news that someone may have hanged themselves in her scullery?

Marjorie paused outside Jasmin's room, wondering whether the unpleasant revelation might be too much for her frail friend. She toyed with the idea of leaving and telling Oscar first. Could she trust him to show sensitivity to his mother if he were to make the disclosure? No. Marjorie thought not. Besides which, she didn't know where Oscar's room was. Jasmin needed to know what had happened.

Taking a deep breath, Marjorie knocked.

And what if it wasn't self-inflicted? the small voice nagged at the back of her mind.

79

Chapter 9

Horace stood at the front door, his heart pounding, more from lack of sleep than the events that had occurred since Marjorie called him. He watched the police pull up in front of the house in a marked car with blue lights flashing but no siren.

The first responder strolled over to have a conversation with the occupants of the car. Then one of the uniformed officers climbed out, gesturing to the ambulance driver, giving permission for them to leave. The first responder paramedic returned to her car and began tapping information on a laptop.

The police officer in the driver's seat remained in the car, speaking into the radio while the other one surveyed the house from the bottom of the steps, walking over to give the limousine a close inspection before climbing up towards Horace. The officer's facial expression beneath the brim of his cap conveyed calm authority.

"Good morning, officer," said Horace, noting as the policeman got closer the worn look on the lined face. The officer removed his hat and rubbed back his dark hair, giving Horace a nod.

"Good morning, sir. Do you live here?"

"No, I'm staying here with friends. I'm Horace Tyler."

"PC Trench. The paramedic told me it was a woman who found the body. Is that right? Is she here?"

"Yes to the first question and no to the second. My friend Lady Marjorie Snellthorpe found the poor gentleman. She won't be long. She's gone to break the news to the owner of the house."

"So this Lady Snellthorpe. Does she live here?"

"Sorry, no. She's one of the friends I mentioned. The house is owned by a gentleman called Oscar Winchester, or it could be his mother, Jasmin Winchester. As I said, Marjorie has gone to speak to the latter. I have seen the deceased, though."

"Can you tell me in your words what happened?" The officer opened his notebook.

"Would you like to come inside?"

PC Trench took a quick glance back towards the patrol car where his colleague was still on the radio. He then turned towards Horace and nodded.

"Yes, thank you."

Horace stepped back from the door so PC Trench could enter. The officer glanced around at the opulent furnishings as he did so.

"It all looks very impressive," he said as they walked together across the hall. "Do you mind if I ask how long you will be staying here?"

"Only until the weekend." Horace felt no need to mention that they had been thinking of leaving this morning. "We have tickets for tennis and Lady Marjorie knows the family."

"Always busy in Wimbledon at this time of year," Trench said. "So, now can you tell me in your own words what happened?"

Horace recounted how Lady Marjorie Snellthorpe had gone to the kitchen in the early hours to get a glass of water and how she had discovered the body hanging in the scullery. He explained how Marjorie had been distressed when she realised it was a corpse, and immediately called for an ambulance and the police before phoning him to come downstairs.

"And neither of you touched anything in the room?"

"No, officer, we didn't."

"Thank you, Mr Tyler. The paramedic also mentioned there was no suicide note found at the scene." The officer emphasised the word suicide, sounding sceptical.

"Did she? Well then, she must be right."

"What? Has she not asked you, or this Lady Snellthorpe, whether either of you found a note?"

Horace remained silent, not wanting to get the paramedic into any trouble. "We didn't find a note."

"My colleague's requesting a supervising sergeant to attend. Now that death has been confirmed, we would like to get the body down as quickly as possible, but there are certain procedures we have to follow. Perhaps you could show me where the dead man is."

"Of course, Officer Trench. Follow me. I'll take you to the scullery."

"And you're certain neither you nor Lady Marjorie touched anything?" Trench enquired.

Horace paused at the top of the stairs. "Marjorie said the man was dead when she found him and she didn't want to contaminate the scene. I only looked in from the door."

"She's trained in that sort of thing, is she, sir?" said Trench.

"Not exactly. But she has seen a dead person before. Besides, she's five-foot-nothing and in her eighties. When you see how high up the fellow is hanging, I think you'll understand."

Horace led the policeman down the steps, following his earlier route. This time, he retrieved the glass of water Marjorie had mentioned from the stairs, not wanting anyone to kick it over. He led PC Trench to the door of the scullery. It was still open from when he'd directed the paramedic inside. Poor Gordon Collins remained suspended from the laundry hanger.

Trench took a step inside, surveying the scene. "Is the room exactly as you found it?"

How many ways can you ask the same question? thought Horace. "Yes. Except the door was closed when Lady Marjorie came down initially."

"Oh, really? What reason did she have for going into the scullery?"

"A cat was scratching at the door, I believe."

"Hmm." Trench moved further inside to get a better view of the body. He hummed as he examined it with clinical detachment, visually checking for any signs of trauma or injury.

Horace took the opportunity to have a closer look at the scullery. It was a modernised Victorian room, with its original exposed brick walls painted a soft cream and terracotta floor tiles. In one corner, there was a large cat bed filled with blankets. A bowl of water sat close by. Next to the cat bed was a tumble dryer, then a washing machine. Nothing seemed out of place other than an overturned stool and Gordon's shoes on the floor.

Officer Trench finished his inspection and said, "I agree with the paramedic. It looks like suicide." His words, though, didn't agree with his face and he put the emphasis on 'looks'. Trench turned back to Horace and asked, "One more question. I got the dead man's name from the paramedic – Gordon Collins. We'll need to have a formal identification, of course, but do you know if he worked here?"

"He's Oscar Winchester's accountant. I only met him last night."

"He didn't live here either?"

"No. I assumed he was staying as there are other guests, but he told us he was going home not long before we went to bed."

"I see. What time was that?"

"Around half-past one."

"Was he working here last night?" PC Trench scribbled a few things down in his notebook.

"I'm not sure. There are other people staying, as I said. Marjorie told me he had come to speak to Oscar."

"Oscar Winchester?"

"Yes."

"And did he?"

"No. Oscar had gone out and didn't return home until after two in the morning. I heard his limousine pull up outside."

"Could Mr Collins have been waiting somewhere in the house after you went to bed?"

Horace rubbed his forehead. "Assuming he didn't come down here and kill himself, Marjorie and I wondered the same thing. It's a big house, so he could have gone anywhere, especially if he was familiar with the place. But why would he say he was leaving if he wasn't?"

"Good question. Well, thank you for your help, Mr Tyler. I'll make a few notes while I'm waiting… While I think of it, is there any other way into this room?"

"There's an external door on the other side of the kitchen," said Horace. "Would you like me to show you?"

"Might as well," said PC Trench.

Once he had shown Trench where the other entrance was and the officer had checked it was locked, Horace was dismissed.

"You go back upstairs now, sir. I may need to talk to you again. In the meantime, if you remember anything or see or hear anything unusual, please let me know. When my sergeant arrives, you can tell him where I am. Someone will also need to speak to Lady Marjorie."

"I'll see if I can find her once your sergeant is here."

PC Trench returned his attention to the room, still making notes in his notebook. "I suggest you wake Mr Winchester and let him know what's happened. We're going to need to cordon off this area of the house until we've assessed the scene. No-one leaves, and nobody, other than my colleagues, is allowed inside the house."

"Right," said Horace, feeling slightly overwhelmed while totting up the number of jobs he had to do. He imagined Edna and Frederick's reaction when they found out they were being held prisoner in Oscar's house – figuratively speaking – until further notice.

Chapter 10

Jasmin's voice sounded distant, but the response was immediate after Marjorie knocked.

"Come in," she called.

When Marjorie opened the door, she found her old friend sitting in the same place she had left her the previous evening. A silhouette of her elegant figure was just visible in the dim light. Jasmin's tousled hair gave an indication of her having been to bed for a short time at least, and she was wearing a cream silk dressing gown, telling Marjorie that she had changed into her nightclothes.

Marjorie stood in the doorway, feeling embarrassed and reticent now she was here. "I'm so sorry to bother you at this unearthly hour," she began.

If Jasmin was surprised by her friend's early visit, she didn't show it. "I take it you couldn't sleep either," she said.

"I forgot to take a glass of water to bed and took the liberty of going down to your kitchen to fetch one. Unfortunately—"

"Come in, Marjorie. Have a seat, my kettle's not long boiled. I can offer you a cup of tea. I was just going to make a pot myself."

Marjorie entered, hesitantly at first, then said, "Why don't I do that?" On reflection, she decided the forthcoming conversation might be better had over a cup of tea. Her tongue stuck to the roof of her mouth, reminding her of how parched she was feeling.

"That would be kind, Marjorie. Everything's in my little kitchenette through that door." Jasmin inclined her head in the direction of the door David had gone through on the previous evening to make hot chocolate.

"Should I pull the curtains?" Marjorie offered. The lack of light gave the room a gloomy atmosphere. Jasmin was sitting in the darkness, with shadows looming in the corners. The news Marjorie was dreading to tell her friend would be gloomy enough without having to reveal it in the dark.

"I'll do that while you make the tea. I'm not quite an invalid," said Jasmin.

Marjorie entered the so-called kitchenette, which was actually a large kitchen, around the same size as Edna's. She was relieved Edna wasn't here, or she might have said something inappropriate. Thinking of what her cousin-in-law might say brought a smile to her face, followed by a frown. Edna would not be pleased with the news of a body hanging in the scullery. At least if Gordon had killed himself, besides being tragic, it would be nothing to concern themselves with.

Marjorie felt guilty dismissing the loss of a man's life in such a disconnected way and hurriedly went about setting the tea tray, which was already laid out. She was pleased to find Jasmin used cups and saucers; her favourite way to take tea.

With tray in hand, she felt a little more cheerful. But when Marjorie returned to the sitting room, her heart sank. Jasmin remained in the exact same position and darkness still shrouded the room. Light from the kitchen illuminated a glazed expression fixed on her friend's face. It wasn't possible to see Jasmin's eyes, but Marjorie suspected they were staring into space. This didn't bode well.

Marjorie ventured forward, setting the tray down on the low table between two armchairs. "Here's our tea," she said.

The clatter of the teacups seemed to break the spell, and Jasmin blinked a few times. Confusion crossed her face for a moment as her head veered towards Marjorie. Within seconds, she appeared to snap back to reality, crossing her hands to regain control.

"Thank you."

Without asking again, Marjorie crossed the room and pulled the heavy drapes apart, allowing the early morning light to dispel the glumness of the room as if by magic. The conservatory windows were open and Marjorie inhaled as she peered out. The sun was rising in all its glory. Purple lavenders, red fuchsias and a colourful array of bedding plants lined the border of a private walled patio. Goldfinches helped themselves to Niger and sunflower seeds hanging from bird feeders while a robin watched on and blackbirds foraged on the border's soil.

"What a beautiful outlook you have here," Marjorie said, returning to sit in the armchair close to Jasmin.

"I had the patio built after Hugh died. It was something we had discussed, and it was my way of commemorating him. It also provides me with my own personal space and a much needed escape. I find all the comings and goings of Oscar and his friends overwhelming at times. The privacy of the patio and the blooms bring solace and a sense of peace."

Although Jasmin sounded stronger and more like her old self, a blankness in the eyes was worrying. Was it loneliness or deep grief? Marjorie knew all about the latter.

She patted her friend's hand before pouring the tea. "Sugar?"

"One spoonful of honey, please."

Marjorie guessed the small china pot with a silver spoon next to it contained honey. Lifting the lid, she discovered her assumption was right. After stirring in the honey, she handed a cup and saucer to her friend.

"I see from the easel in your conservatory you're a talented artist," she said, taking a sip from her own cup and concluding it might be better not to say what she had been intending to.

"I've always enjoyed painting, and it helps pass the time. The days can be so long at this time of year." The two women settled facing each other, sipping tea while Marjorie offered refills from the pot. They talked of the past, of friends they had known, of sorrows and joys, of life and love.

"If it wasn't for David, I don't know how I would go on," Jasmin said. "Do you ever wonder what the point of it all is?" She waved her free hand around the room.

Alarm bells rang again. This wasn't the woman Marjorie had known, nor even the person she had been speaking to last night who, apart from the funny turn, had been much more upbeat. Although Marjorie could relate to the occasional bout of moroseness since Ralph had passed, she wasn't one to allow such feelings to overwhelm her.

"There's still a lot to live for, Jasmin," she said softly, while reaching out a comforting hand and lightly rubbing her friend's arm. "You have Oscar and David. Your garden is lovely and, as you say, your painting keeps you occupied."

Jasmin nodded, then took another sip of tea before continuing in a more relaxed tone. "I love the garden in the summer. We get so many varieties of bees here. I paint, you know?"

Marjorie recoiled again, wondering whether Jasmin was suffering from some form of dementia. "Yes, I saw the outline of a portrait on the easel," she said.

"I get a lot of pleasure from painting."

"Who is the portrait of?"

"I'm hoping to recreate a memory of David from when he was younger."

"Did he marry?"

"No. He says he never got over his first love, whoever that might be. He doesn't say."

Marjorie suspected she knew who, but said nothing.

"Are portraits your specialism?"

"Not at all. I usually paint animals and birds, but I've got a book on portraiture and wanted to give it a go. If it turns out to be any good, I'll give it to David for his birthday. It is lovely to see you again, Marjorie, but I fear I might have cut you off earlier. You mentioned something happened when you went to fetch a glass of water. Please don't worry if you broke a glass. We have plenty."

Marjorie swallowed a lump in her throat and placed her cup and saucer back down on the tray.

"It wasn't a broken glass, Jasmin. I'm sorry to tell you, but something happened to Mr Collins."

Jasmin eyed her teacup with a disbelieving stare. "Gordon? Did he speak to Oscar? I do hope Oscar hasn't fired him; his outbursts can be so rash when he gets upset. I don't know where he gets his temper from. Hugh was such a calm man."

Marjorie shook her head, feeling solemn. "I don't think Gordon was able to speak to Oscar and as far as I'm aware, he wasn't dismissed," she said, although she didn't know whether either of those assumptions were true. "He's… I suppose there's only one way to put this. Gordon Collins is dead."

Jasmin's hands trembled as she poured herself another cup of tea. "Would you like one?" she asked Marjorie in a monotone voice.

Marjorie hesitated for a moment before nodding. "Thank you."

"Gordon's dead, you say? Did he have a car accident? No. Of course not. You said something happened in the kitchen. Was it a heart attack?"

"It wasn't a heart attack and he wasn't in the kitchen. I found him in the scullery."

"But that's Casper's room. Is Casper all right?"

Marjorie eyed Jasmin curiously. This was going to be even harder than she had imagined, but she felt it better not to reveal everything all at once.

"Is Casper a ginger tom?"

"Yes, he loathes surprises."

Marjorie felt an eyebrow rise and gave a faint smile. "You'll be pleased to hear Casper is quite all right. It was he who led me to open the scullery door in the first place. I'm sorry to bring you such terrible news."

"The door to the scullery is always open. We never close it. Not that I venture down there very much these days. Everyone knows it's Casper's room, and it really is a pain to open the door if closed. It catches on the tiles."

"It was difficult to open, I grant you, but closed it was. Alas, when I opened it, I found Mr Collins hanging from the laundry dryer." Marjorie didn't mention Casper taking flight or ask about the black cat, wondering whether the latter had been a figment of her imagination.

The crash of the teacup was loud because it hit the coffee table on its way to the floor. Marjorie watched the tea spreading on the cream rug while patting her friend's hand and face to prevent her from fainting.

Chapter 11

A second police car pulled up outside and a burly officer got out. The newcomer had a quick word with the man still sitting in the other car. Horace wondered if he always left his partner to do all the legwork or whether they took turns; he had shown no desire to come inside and inspect the crime scene. The new arrival had sergeant stripes on his shoulders, Horace noticed while the man walked up to where he was.

"I'm Sergeant Baker. I take it you're Mr Tyler?"

"I am, sergeant."

"Please lead the way."

The sergeant, a man of few words, dismissed Horace once he had showed him to the scullery. Horace hovered at the foot of the stairs for a few minutes, listening to

Trench relaying the snippets of information he had gleaned from him and the paramedic.

"So, what are your thoughts, then, Billy?" Sergeant Baker asked.

"It's a strange one, sir. First, there's the lack of a suicide note… then there's the rope."

"What about it?"

"It doesn't belong here, although the deceased could have brought it with him, I suppose. If so, that would suggest he planned to commit suicide, which would make it even more peculiar. Why would a bloke who doesn't even live in this place choose it as the one to come and hang himself?"

"Perhaps he didn't like the owner," Baker replied.

"Even so," Trench said.

"We'll need to confirm the dead man's ID. From what you've gathered so far, he's the house owner's accountant?"

"That's what I've been told. I've asked Kenny to run the name through the usual channels for next of kin and so on. It's unclear whether this house belongs to Mr Oscar Winchester or his mother. Either way, if the deceased was their accountant, what was he doing in the scullery? It's hardly somewhere he'd have been familiar with. And if he did want to make a point, why not hang himself somewhere in the main house? He could have thrown himself off the first-floor balcony. It's high enough to kill a man who jumped and strong enough to have done the deed if he'd used the same rope."

"I'm inclined to agree with your line of thinking. It can't have been an accident, but it could still be suicide, or a murder made to look like a suicide. In the latter case, we're looking at someone trying to hide that fact. I'd like to get him down from there and take a look at that knot."

"Are you sure we should do that?" Trench asked.

"We could lower him via this old washing hanger without disturbing the scene too much. But, perhaps you're right. Let's get the CSI team in to take photos first, and do what they do best. I'll refer it to Major Crimes and let them decide where to go from here."

Horace heard a sound coming from the upstairs hall and felt he'd risked lingering for long enough. He climbed the steps, almost tripping over a cat.

"Where did you come from?" Horace whispered, picking up the ginger moggy. He waited a few moments to make sure neither the sergeant nor PC Trench had heard him, but the sergeant's voice on the radio requesting the Major Crimes team told him they were otherwise engaged.

By the time Horace got to the hall, there was no-one to be seen. Perhaps it had been one of the guys in white he'd heard moving around. Horace placed the cat on the floor.

"If I were you, Ginger, I'd stay out of the way," he said, giving the animal a stroke. The cat responded by purring and rubbing his fur against Horace's legs.

"Where have you been? I've been banging on your door and phoning you and Marge for the past half an hour," Edna hissed, tiptoeing down the stairs. "Are we leaving or what?"

Horace took a quick look around. "I must have left my phone in my room. I'm afraid to say there's been a change of plan."

Edna's face darkened. "I'm not staying in this house another night. I hardly slept a wink." She had reached Horace now, and her raised voice sent the ginger cat scarpering through the open front door. She stared after him. "Where did that come from, and why's the front door open at this time in the morning?"

Horace took Edna's arm. "Not here. Come with me and I'll explain everything. Then I need to speak to Oscar. Do you know which room he's in?"

"How should I know? I'm not his keeper," Edna moaned, but followed Horace along the hall, past the ornamental sabres to the room where they had spent the previous evening.

"In here." Horace opened the door, hoping for a quiet tête-à-tête, but found David Cribb in earnest conversation with the dour Jamie.

David's head shot up, and he forced a smile. "Good morning. I trust you slept well."

"Not bad, thank you," Horace lied. "I'm sorry, we didn't realise anyone else was up." He tried to back out, but Edna was already pushing past him into the room.

"How was your night?" David asked her.

"Erm, it could have been better," she said. "Strange bed and all that… you know how it is."

"I hope the racket in the early hours didn't disturb you." David glared at Jamie.

"I just do as I'm told," Jamie retorted.

"If only that were true."

"I've already told you—"

"There's been an incident," Horace interrupted. "Didn't you notice the police cars outside?"

"Police? Here? Why?" David's forehead creased.

Horace noticed Jamie's hand moving to his inside jacket pocket. The gun he had been carrying yesterday was bulging from a holster.

"I suggest you get rid of that thing before you're arrested," said Horace.

"Do as he says," David instructed.

Horace watched Jamie reluctantly leaving them to dispose of his weapon.

"Why is he still carrying that gun?" Edna asked. "I thought Oscar was going to tell him to put it away. He deserves what he gets if someone's snitched on him."

"No, Edna. That's not why the police are here," said Horace.

David appeared surprised. "I think you had better explain what's going on," he said.

Horace closed the door and moved Edna to a chair. "I'm sorry to tell you, but Marjorie found a man hanging in the scullery in the early hours of this morning. It's Gordon Collins."

Edna's mouth opened and closed a few times while David appeared to be processing what he had just heard.

"Is he dead?" she asked.

"Yes," said Horace.

"Suicide?" David asked.

Horace shrugged, not wanting to disclose what he had overheard in case David was implicated. "That's what it looks like. The police are downstairs now and Marjorie has gone to inform Jasmin. She's been a while."

"Excuse me," said David, racing to the door and scurrying away.

Edna shook her head. "By the look on your face, Horace Tyler, it ain't no bloomin' suicide," she said.

"I overheard the police having a discussion. They believe the death's suspicious and are calling in their Major Crimes team."

"Get me a glass of water, will you?" Edna said. "I've got a splitting headache."

Horace did as bid and Edna retrieved some paracetamol tablets from her handbag, downing two at once, followed by a slurp of water. After she had gulped down the rest of the water, she handed him the empty glass. Horace refilled it and sat down next to her.

"Even if the police let us leave, which is questionable after what they said to me initially…" watching Edna's face fall, he added, "For today at least… I don't think Marjorie will want to go now. She's worried about her old friend."

"Why would anyone kill an innocuous accountant? Are you sure it's not suicide? He seemed a bit on edge last night. Maybe he had trouble at home."

"I'm surprised you noticed what state he was in last night." Horace patted her hand. "I thought he appeared happy enough – not like a man about to kill himself."

"Okay. So, I'd had a few, but I wasn't out of my bloomin' mind. You might not have noticed, but I did. That guy was worried about something. Maybe he mucked up Oscar's accounts and decided he couldn't face his boss after all. Let's face it, Oscar Winchester hardly strikes me as the forgiving type."

"Did you hear Oscar come home last night? I'm assuming that's the racket David was referring to just now."

"No, I was fast asleep."

Horace smirked. "You just told me you didn't sleep a wink."

"Maybe I got a few hours, but I was still hoping we'd be out of here this morning. What sort of racket? Did it sound like someone was murdering the accountant?"

Laughing, Horace said, "Nothing like that. Just car doors slamming. I saw Oscar and Jamie having a bit of a row, and then I heard Oscar pass my room on his way to bed. I don't think he had time to speak to Gordon Collins, let alone hang him up in the scullery. We all thought he'd gone home, remember?" Horace jumped up. "That reminds me, the policeman I spoke to asked me to let Oscar know what's happened. I should have asked David where his room is."

Edna rubbed her forehead. "I wouldn't worry about that. Jamie will get him up as soon as he's hidden his gun. I can't work him out, can you?"

"Jamie or David? Seeing them in here makes me wonder who's really the boss around here. But Jamie doesn't know what happened, so why would he wake Oscar?"

"Ah, but are you sure about that? Even if he was worried about possessing an illegal weapon, he seemed uncharacteristically uninquisitive when you said there'd been an incident involving the police. He didn't even ask what it was."

"I expect that's because he jumped to the same conclusion you did and thought someone had told the police about his gun. And he seemed to have been given a rollicking by David, so maybe he didn't want to push his luck."

"Maybe, but David doesn't employ him, Oscar does." Edna straightened the new blonde wig. "Or maybe he already knew what it was about because he had done away with the accountant for Oscar."

Horace grinned. "While you're in the mood for hypotheses," he put his hand out to help her up, "let's see what we can find out."

Edna took the offered hand, frowning. "I don't see why we should need to find out anything. I want to watch tennis."

"Now I know you're lying. The least we can do is to check whether Oscar knows what's happened under his roof. Plus, the policeman asked me to let Marjorie know they wanted to speak to her."

"Trust her to go and find a dead body in the middle of the night," Edna complained.

Chapter 12

With a thunderous crash, David Cribb burst into Jasmin's room. He was panting from the exertion.

His wild eyes told Marjorie all she needed to know. He had heard the news.

"How are you?" With heavy footsteps, he hurried over to Jasmin, taking her hand in his.

Jasmin scrunched her eyes, her face pale, as if trying to remember what had happened. She looked up at him with a tired expression.

"Here, drink this." Marjorie handed her a glass of water.

"You shouldn't have troubled her." David glared at Marjorie. "Jasmin's got enough on her plate. This is none of your business."

Jasmin straightened, withdrawing her hand from David's grasp. "I had to know, David," she said firmly.

"Marjorie is treating me like an adult... unlike so many people in this house. This is still my home."

David's eyes dropped to the floor. Sighing, he said, "Of course. I apologise, Lady Marjorie." He turned his attention back to Jasmin. "I worry about you, that's all."

As well you might, Marjorie thought, but said, "Now you're here, I expect the police would like to interview me. Please excuse me."

David walked her to the door, his face a mixture of emotions.

"What's happening here?" Marjorie asked quietly. "How long has Jasmin been having these vacant episodes? Has she seen a doctor?"

He cleared his throat, shifting from one foot to the other. "It's nothing to worry about. She gets better later in the day. I tend to her in the mornings until she's ready to face the crowds. This is how she wants it."

"I see. Did the police tell you about Mr Collins?"

"No, I haven't seen the police. All I know is what your friends Horace and Edna told me. I came here as soon as I heard. What would drive him to commit suicide in this house? I thought he'd left."

"That's the precise question the police will want answered, I'm sure."

"David?" Jasmin called.

"I'm just coming," he said.

"Do you know where my friends are now?" asked Marjorie.

"They were in the entertainment lounge."

"The entertainment lounge?"

"Where we were last night. That's where I left them. Look, I'd better go. Sorry about before."

"Think nothing of it." Marjorie left, not entirely satisfied with David's explanation about her old friend's health, but if it was Jasmin's choice not to seek help, or if she had and wanted to keep her diagnosis a secret, then it wasn't really any of Marjorie's business.

She turned a corner just in time to see Horace and Edna exiting the entertainment lounge. Edna saw her first.

"I can't believe you, Marge," she snapped.

"I should have stayed in bed, but I was so thirsty."

"You always do this to us."

Open-mouthed, Marjorie couldn't believe her ears. "This situation is hardly my fault, Edna."

"Don't mind Edna, she's in shock," said Horace.

And I'm hardly dancing for joy, thought Marjorie, pursing her lips lest she say something she might regret.

"How did your mate Jasmin take the news?" Edna asked.

"Not well, but I don't think we should talk here. Too many ears." Marjorie inclined her head towards the shorter of the men in white, who was heading their way. He addressed Marjorie.

"Mr Winchester would like to see you in the morning room."

Where on earth is the morning room? Marjorie wondered, but didn't ask. "And I would very much like to speak to Mr Winchester. But first, I must wash and change," she replied.

The man's face darkened. His eyes were sharp. Marjorie had no doubt he was about to insist, but Horace jumped in.

"Lady Marjorie has been up half the night and has had quite a shock. We all have. I'm sure Oscar will understand when you explain. I suggest we meet for a chat over breakfast in an hour. Where is the dining room, by the way?"

"Erm—"

"Don't worry. We'll find it. Come along, ladies."

The trio left the bewildered man scratching his head. Edna grinned.

"I hate to admit it, but you come in handy sometimes, Horace Tyler."

"I'll take that as a compliment, Mrs Parkinton," said Horace, preening.

"Before we go back downstairs, let's have a meetup in my room in half an hour," said Marjorie. "Has anyone told Frederick what's going on?"

"Edna phoned him just before we ran into you," said Horace.

"Oh dear. I don't expect he was happy."

"Understatement, Marge, but I'm not ecstatic about the news myself, so why's he so special?"

"Because he's a more tender soul," said Horace, taking Edna's arm while they climbed the stairs.

"Humph. Just because I don't make a fuss about everything doesn't mean I don't feel it."

Marjorie bit her tongue in order to prevent herself from commenting on the fact Edna had been doing just that since they met downstairs, not to mention the many other times Edna had made a fuss about trivial things as well as important ones.

When they arrived outside her room, Marjorie inserted the key into the keyhole. Edna gasped.

"How come you've got a key?"

"There are keys in all the doors, Edna," said Horace. "Come with me, I'll show you. We'll be with you soon, Marjorie. Once I've sorted the duchess here, I'll let Fred in on the plan."

Horace led a complaining Edna next door while Marjorie entered her bedroom, shaking her head. After closing it, she stood for a few minutes with her back to the door, taking deep breaths to calm herself after the unsettling events of the past few hours.

***

Frederick's face was pale and drawn as he arrived at Marjorie's door, Edna and Horace following close behind. Horace appeared determined. Edna had changed wigs from blonde to purple. Marjorie had deduced that Edna wore the purple wig when she needed confidence, almost like a rebellious teenager might use outlandish clothes to bolster their self-esteem.

Marjorie was grateful for the lavish room with ample furniture so they could all sit in comfort. Frederick had barely spoken since arriving, and Marjorie sympathised. He was a man who didn't like drama, preferring peace and quiet, but since he'd met Marjorie, he had been catapulted into several murder investigations, even being a suspect in one.

"I don't think we've got long." Horace broke the silence. "The big man in white is hovering on the landing. I don't think he'll be as easily fobbed off as the other one."

Marjorie nodded understanding. "In that case, let's go over what we know so far. There's something highly suspicious about these goings on. I hope the police aren't too quick to jump to conclusions on the suicide front."

"Let me reassure you on that score, Marjorie. The officer I met, PC Trench, is a sensible fellow, and he's not convinced Gordon killed himself. I overheard him speaking with a sergeant who was called in—"

"He means he was eavesdropping," said Edna.

"I admit to hovering close to the scullery a little longer than necessary," said Horace, grinning. "Anyway, Trench thought the rope seemed out of place, just like you did, Marjorie."

Marjorie felt her face flush as Edna and Frederick turned questioning eyes towards her.

"It didn't appear to be in keeping with the clothes dryer," she explained.

"Like that makes any sense!" Edna spluttered.

"It makes perfect sense to me," said Horace. "Along with that, there was the lack of a suicide note—"

"I hadn't thought to look for a note," Marjorie interrupted.

"Just goes to show you don't know everything, Marge," said Edna.

Ignoring Edna, Marjorie asked Horace, "Did this PC Trench say anything else?"

"The place of death didn't make any sense to him, either. Why would Gordon kill himself in Oscar

Winchester's home and why do the deed in the scullery? When I had to leave, they were calling in Major Crimes."

"Why did you have to leave?" Frederick asked.

"I heard sounds coming from the hallway. Then I almost tripped over a cat."

"That would be Casper."

Edna raised her eyebrows at Marjorie. "I take it Casper is the ginger thing that shot out the door when I came along."

"The one you startled with your shouting."

Marjorie got the picture.

"Anyway," Horace continued, "I expect the Major Crime squad will be here by now."

"And the PC told Horace they want to speak to you, Marge." Edna actually looked sympathetic for a change.

"It must have been quite a shock finding him in there like that." Frederick's eyes were soft as he looked at her. Marjorie hadn't had enough time to take the whole tragedy in, apart from the few moments' silence before she took a shower and changed her clothes, but she felt her heart banging in her chest now that things had slowed down.

"The poor man," she said. "I hope the police have brought him down from there."

"May I suggest we leave once the police have interviewed you?" Frederick said.

"And Horace," said Edna. "He saw the body too, you know. They'll want to speak to him."

"I've already spoken to PC Trench," Horace said, "and I'm afraid he said no-one is to leave the house."

"I wouldn't leave Jasmin anyway," said Marjorie.

"Oh, come on, Marge, do us all a favour," Edna complained. "You haven't seen the woman for years."

"Something I'm regretting," said Marjorie, her face determined.

"Well, I'm not sure about this. What about the tennis?"

Marjorie couldn't help but chuckle. "I'm surprised you're arguing from that perspective. You said you didn't enjoy the sport."

"If it's a choice between watching men in shorts smacking a ball over a net and staying in this place with Jamie and his gun, the weird men in white, grey, pink or whatever, and your mate Oscar, I'll take the tennis."

Marjorie roared with laughter. Horace also burst out laughing and when Edna didn't join in, he laid a comforting hand on her shoulder.

Once she stopped laughing, Marjorie said, "It's difficult to explain, but there's something strange going on here."

"You'll get no argument from me on that point," said Edna.

"Why are you worried about Jasmin?" Frederick asked. "Isn't this more likely to have something to do with Oscar and his cronies?"

"I wish I could explain. I just need a little more time, that's all—"

"Here we go," said Edna. "She's got that look in her eyes."

"Marjorie's instincts are good," said Horace. "Let's see what the police make of the accountant's death and give Marjorie time to be more certain about her friend's safety."

Grateful to Horace for his support, Marjorie was delighted when the others agreed.

"In which case," she said, "I suggest we get started."

"Over breakfast," said Edna. "I'm starving."

Chapter 13

Oscar's face was red with rage and he waved his arms while yelling at the stocky man in white in the hallway. When he caught sight of Marjorie and the others descending the stairs, Oscar stopped mid-sentence, his arms dropping to his sides. Marjorie felt a pang of guilt as the man scurried away, no doubt hoping to escape punishment for her failing to heed his boss's earlier call.

"Ah, Lady Marjorie and friends, how good to see you! I'm sorry you didn't sleep well. I hear you've had quite a night."

The effusive greeting and attempt at making light of the situation came across as exaggerated. "Good morning, Oscar. I apologise for not being able to see you earlier. As you say, it had been an eventful few hours."

He waved the apology away. "Think nothing of it. Under the circumstances, I understand. If you're ready now, perhaps you would join me and the others for breakfast."

Marjorie glanced sideways at the police cordon blocking the entrance to the lower floor, and therefore the kitchen. "We would be delighted," she said.

"This way, please." After his staccato command, Oscar about-turned and crossed the main hallway before opening a door to the right. They had yet to have a tour of the house and its many rooms. Horace raised an eyebrow at Marjorie, but they remained quiet.

The quartet followed their host into an immense banqueting room. An extensive unlaid table ran through the middle of the room and a grand fireplace took centre stage on the wall. Marjorie would have loved to pause and imagine the conversations that may have taken place at this very table with a blazing fire affording its guests warmth. There was no time for reflection, however. Oscar was in a hurry. They followed him at a pace past the table.

"Look at those cornices and the coving," said Frederick during the route march.

"I was admiring the chandeliers," said Horace.

Marjorie glimpsed both. The Victorian architectural ceilings with floral plaster cornices and decorative coving were in keeping with the style of the room. Two chandeliers hung from matching plaster ceiling roses.

After arriving at the far end of the room, Oscar led them through a set of double doors into a smaller dining room where the rest of the party were milling around, looking agitated.

Edna nudged Marjorie. "This setup is like the formal areas in your house, except a lot grander."

"And about three times the size," said Marjorie.

Oscar stopped abruptly, not giving Edna time to apply her brakes. She almost fell into him.

"Give us some warning, mate," she cried, before putting a hand to her mouth.

"My apologies, Edna," said Oscar, grinning at her outburst. Marjorie hoped the fact their host clearly liked Edna's straight talking would come in handy.

Terry Kemble cleared his throat behind Oscar, whose head spun around.

"Sorry to interrupt, but I have to go out. I've got a meeting this morning."

"I'm not keeping you here, Terry. The police are." Oscar waved a dismissive hand. "Come and sit down, Lady Marjorie."

"Marjorie, please."

"As you wish," said Oscar. "I apologise for the melodrama, but the police have barred us from the kitchen and requested that we all remain in the house for now. I'm not sure if you'll be able to make it to the tennis today." Oscar's tone was friendly, but his eyes were like flint when he made a show of pulling a dining chair out for her. Her friends were beside her in a flash, Frederick taking a seat to her right while Horace and Edna hurried around to the other side of the table to sit opposite. Their care of her made Marjorie feel safe.

"Thank you, Oscar," she said politely. "The police have already informed Horace that no-one is to leave, so we were expecting this."

Oscar sat himself in the chair to her left. "Please sit down, all of you," he said to his other guests. "Breakfast will be here shortly." He turned back to Marjorie. "I've had to request a catering delivery because of the excitement downstairs. It's just while the police and forensics team finish what they are doing. So hopefully, it's a temporary measure."

Terry sat next to Edna, fidgeting with his tie in between drumming his fingers on the table. Paris Toliver took the seat opposite Oscar.

"It had better be," she snapped, "or I'll have words." Her tone was threatening and her face determined. Did Marjorie mistake an increased pulsation in Oscar's temple? She wasn't sure.

"They have to do their job, Paris. Let's all be patient, shall we?"

"I don't like being kept prisoner. What was your accountant doing down there in the first place? Terry says he told everyone he was going home."

Oscar tried to shrug away her concern with a half-smile, but the subtle shifting of his jaw revealed he was far from relaxed. His frequent swallowing also betrayed underlying tension.

"Apparently he didn't go home. Did you see him leave, Terry?"

"No. I just assumed he did what he said he was going to do. As far as I'm aware, there would be no reason for him to sneak about the house after we went to bed, which I did at the same time as Horace and Edna."

"And he didn't tell you what he wanted to see me about?"

"Nope. Just said he had some business to discuss with you. Your mother assumed you'd forgotten to sign something again. It wouldn't be the first time." Terry attempted a half-laugh.

"Where is Jasmin?" Marjorie asked.

"David's looking after her. They'll have breakfast in her room. She hasn't been feeling well. It might have been better if she hadn't known about the incident." Oscar's eyes held Marjorie's, dark and accusatory.

"I hardly think you could have kept the apparent suicide of one of your friends a secret for long," Horace intervened. "Better she know now than find out later."

Oscar didn't say anything. Jamie appeared behind him and whispered something in his ear.

"Breakfast is on its way. I'm sure we'll all feel better when we have some food inside of us." He turned to Jamie. "Tell them to bring it in as soon as it arrives."

"I'm pleased to see he's got rid of the weapon," said Edna, glaring after the bodyguard.

"Boys and their toys," said Oscar. "Rest assured, dear Edna, the gun isn't even loaded. I keep the bullets locked away."

"That's reassuring," said Marjorie. "Will Georgina be joining us?"

Oscar's neck flashed red and he flinched. "My wife is keeping to her room. She's found the whole thing distressing."

"Yeah, very," Paris sniped.

"Unlike some people, Paris, Georgina is sensitive."

"If you say so."

Marjorie wondered whether Paris was always confrontational or whether she was still annoyed at Oscar for making a fool of her the day before.

The men in white brought breakfast through and laid three generously portioned platters of food on the table.

The food looked appetising, but Marjorie wasn't overjoyed with the hot drinks served in cardboard cartons. There wasn't a choice, either.

"I'm afraid it's coffee or coffee," said Oscar when the taller man in white placed a carton in front of Marjorie.

"I'll have coffee, then." She smiled at the unflinching man. "Thank you."

Edna gave Marjorie a knowing look, unable to keep the smirk off her face. "Marge loves coffee on the go, don't you, Marge?"

Marjorie grinned when Horace nudged Edna, mouthing, "Behave."

"We could ask Jasmin for a pot of tea, if you prefer?" Paris offered.

Marjorie was sorely tempted, but shook her head. "Coffee is fine. It might wake me up."

"So, who found the body?" Paris asked Oscar. He inclined his head towards Marjorie. Paris's eyes widened.

"What were you doing downstairs in the early hours?" Oscar asked Marjorie before stuffing half of a hot bacon roll into his mouth in one go. Marjorie found herself hungry after her exertions, but wasn't a fan of bacon butties. She helped herself to cheese, salami and bread from the platter in front of her.

"I woke up thirsty and couldn't find a glass, so I went to fetch a glass of water."

"You could have called for one of these two. Didn't they tell you about the pull cords?" He glared at the men in white who hovered behind Horace. She hadn't been told, but she wouldn't have used the cord anyway, so it was immaterial.

"I wouldn't presume to call people in the middle of the night unless there was an emergency."

Oscar laughed. "I had the cords restored, so they're all in working order. What about you, Edna? Would you have called for help?"

Edna had her mouth full of bread roll, so she just gave him a wag of the finger for teasing.

"So you went to get a glass of water from the scullery?" Paris's eyes were sceptical.

"No, I—"

"Could someone pass me down the fry-up? I'm not into this continental stuff," Edna said, turning her nose up at the cheese platter.

One of the men in white swapped the platters around. Edna and Horace helped themselves to a full English breakfast.

"You were saying…" Paris glowered at Edna before turning back to Marjorie.

"I didn't know there was a scullery. Johnson brought us in through the kitchen last night when we arrived back from our day out. I don't make a habit of wandering around my host's kitchen," she looked at Oscar. "Anyway, I found a glass and was on my way back upstairs with the water when I heard Casper scratching at the scullery door."

"I was calling him Ginger before you told us his name," said Horace.

"And I called him Mr Tom—"

Paris rolled her eyes and Edna gave Marjorie a 'get on with it' look.

"He's my mother's cat," said Oscar. "Are you saying the scullery door was closed? We don't close it. It gets stuck." He glowered at the men in white again.

"It was open when we went upstairs," the taller of the two said.

"And what time was that?" Oscar fired back.

The taller man checked with the shorter, who said, "Just after we showed your guests to the entertainment lounge. David told us we wouldn't be needed again."

Marjorie felt sorry for the two men. Dour they may be, but they didn't deserve to be cross-examined in front of a table of people.

She continued her story. "Jasmin told me you usually keep it open, but I can assure you it was closed. It took some effort on my part to push it open, and when I finally got there, we saw Mr Collins."

"We?" Paris asked.

"Casper and I," said Marjorie, "except he ran off. I thought I caught sight of a black cat running from the scullery, but I may have imagined it."

"That would have been Ben. He belongs to Alison, the house manager. He sneaks in sometimes when Casper's not looking."

"House manager?" Paris chortled. "Glorified housekeeper is what she is."

Marjorie wasn't sure she liked Paris Toliver and was beginning to understand why Oscar might want to put her in her place occasionally. "After seeing poor Mr Collins hanging there, I called for an ambulance, and then Horace. He's always reliable in a crisis."

"Perhaps you should have called your host," said Paris.

"I wasn't thinking straight and didn't know which room the Winchesters slept in. I'd heard a car arriving late and assumed Oscar and Georgina would be fast asleep."

Paris huffed. "And were you both fast asleep?"

"Georgina had a headache. She slept in her room. I expect we were both asleep at the time Marjorie found Gordon."

"Why would he do such a thing? Why kill himself?" Terry quizzed. "He seemed okay when I was talking to him."

"He didn't kill himself, sir," a voice cut in from the doorway. Oscar and the others looked around, fear palpable in the air. "Your accountant was murdered."

Chapter 14

Marjorie recognised the newcomer from her holiday with her friends in the Scottish Highlands the year before. Tall and attractive with wild shoulder-length blonde hair, DI Patricia Bloom was accompanied by a fresh-faced, lanky young man who looked like he was just out of school. Marjorie knew the DI recognised her and her friends, but her poker face was giving nothing away. Edna opened her mouth to speak, but Marjorie noticed Horace giving her a gentle poke in the ribs, shaking his head at the same time.

Oscar's face had turned a dark shade of purple. "That's not possible… how can a man be murdered under my roof?"

DI Bloom scanned the table before looking him in the eye. "And you are?"

Oscar pushed his chair back, standing and making an unsuccessful attempt at squaring up to the detective, who was taller than he was. It brought to mind Horace's description of Oscar jabbing a finger at the enormous Jamie in the early hours. If it hadn't been so serious a matter, Marjorie would have cackled. Edna couldn't resist a smirk.

"My name is Oscar Winchester, and this is my home. Where's the sergeant I spoke to earlier? Who are you?"

"The case has been handed over to me now, sir. I'm Detective Inspector Patricia Bloom from the Major Investigations Team. This is Detective Constable Imran Sudhik and my sergeant, DS Blaby, is on the premises, as is the CSI team. I realise it's difficult to comprehend, but I regret to inform you we are treating the deceased's death as murder until proven otherwise."

The inspector paused while her words hung in the air.

The room was so silent that all anyone could hear were Oscar's shallow breaths and the ticking of the clock on the wall. Oscar's expression was one of disbelief and confusion. His eyes widened as he absorbed the detective's words. His mouth was slightly open as he attempted to take in the situation's gravity.

DI Bloom broke the silence. "I would like to interview everyone in the house, starting with the person who found the body."

Marjorie felt the eyes of most of those present boring into her before she spoke up. "I'm Marjorie Snellthorpe. I found the body, Inspector."

"Is there a room we can use, Mr Winchester?" DI Bloom looked once more at Oscar. He held on to the back of a dining chair before snapping into action.

"Show the inspector to my sitting room, Jamie," he ordered.

Marjorie saw the bodyguard tense.

"I've been informed that most people in the room don't live here," said DI Bloom. "Please, could you let DC Sudhik have details of everyone who was in the house last night, starting with names and addresses? I'd rather no-one leave until I've had the chance to interview them."

Terry Kemble threw his napkin down on the table. "Look, Inspector. Whilst I'm sorry to hear of Gordon's death, and realise you have a job to do, I have an important business meeting to attend this morning." His eyes were pleading.

"Who are you, sir?" DI Bloom asked.

"Terry Kemble."

"Ah, yes." DI Bloom exchanged a knowing glance with her constable. "You manage the European chain of hotels. We'll interview you after Mrs Snellthorpe, then you can go."

"It's *Lady* Snellthorpe," said Oscar.

"I beg your pardon." Bloom nodded at Marjorie. "Shall we go?"

The two women followed Jamie to Oscar's sitting room. Having opened the door, Oscar's bodyguard retreated, giving Marjorie the impression he couldn't leave fast enough. It seemed an age since she and her friends had witnessed Paris Toliver flying from this very room in a rage the day before.

Once the door closed, both women smiled at each other.

"Why the secrecy?" Marjorie asked.

"As you are not under suspicion, we wouldn't want to play all our cards at this early stage. You never know; the *awesome foursome* might come in handy. I wouldn't want our killer… or killers to suspect you're anything more than a bunch of innocuous elderly tourists. The sergeant told my team you're here for the tennis."

Marjorie sighed heavily. "We are, or were. It appears our plans might have changed somewhat. You gathered a lot of information in such a short space of time. I'm impressed."

"PC Trench spoke to Horace earlier when you'd skedaddled off." She grinned. "He's a good copper and takes excellent notes."

"But how did you know who Terry Kemble was? I'm only just finding out who these people are myself."

"Terence Kemble has been pestering the team ever since we arrived. My sergeant had to stop him from leaving, and then from crossing the crime scene. As you know, we are ultra-protective of our crime scenes!"

Marjorie chuckled, recollecting how she and Horace had crossed DI Bloom's crime scene the previous year. "On that note, what brings you down to London? You seemed settled in the Scottish Highlands the last time we met."

"My husband was offered a promotion down here, so I applied for a job in the Met. There are always vacancies and they need to up their quota of women DIs, so I got the job."

Marjorie hadn't even realised the DI was married. She checked her left hand, which confirmed she didn't wear a wedding ring.

"I'm sure you got the job on merit, Inspector Bloom, not to fulfil anyone's quota."

DI Bloom grinned again, flicking her unruly curls behind her ears. "Perhaps. Now, I've already been given a brief summary of what happened in the early hours, but could you walk me through it in your own words? I have some question over the times."

Marjorie recounted everything, from going to bed and hearing other people returning to their rooms and the arrival of cars in the early hours. She then explained how she had gone down to the kitchen to get the ill-fated glass of water and how the ginger cat, Casper, had drawn her attention to the scullery door.

"The odd thing, and I suppose this fits in with your murder theory, is that everyone I've spoken to so far says the door to the scullery is never closed, so unless Gordon Collins shut himself in, the killer must have closed it on leaving. I'm afraid that's all I can tell you."

"At what time did you hear Mr Winchester's car?" Bloom asked.

"I couldn't be certain. Horace will be able to tell you more about that. He witnessed Oscar and his bodyguard, Jamie, having words when they got back. He also saw the body, as you know. I called him after phoning for an ambulance and requesting the police. What makes you sure the death wasn't suicide?"

"Several things, which I'm sure you've picked up on, knowing how sharp your brain is. The lack of a suicide note, the crime scene being an unusual place, the rope and his being here to meet with Oscar Winchester. Why would he kill himself before seeing him, and how can we be certain he didn't?"

"I see your point, Inspector. We thought the rope unusual and I couldn't help wondering why he took his shoes off."

"Unless he kicked them off in a struggle, you mean?" DI Bloom asked.

"I'm not sure what I meant. It just seemed odd."

"Well, between you and me, and because I know I can count on your discretion, the pathologist's initial findings suggest someone tied the knot for him, and that he was most likely strangled before being hanged to hide the fact. If she's right, it was all a rather a clumsy effort to cover up a crime, so it might not have been premeditated."

"Interesting about the knot," said Marjorie. "It's always fascinating what one can discover after death."

"The knot in the rope was tied in a way that suggests somebody else did it. I'll know a lot more later, but we have enough evidence to investigate it as murder. Did you speak to the deceased or see anything out of the ordinary last night?"

"I'm afraid not. I was tired, and my only conversation was with Jasmin, Oscar's mother – she's an old friend. She had a funny turn, so David Cribb – I think he lives here – and Frederick helped me take her to her room. Jasmin didn't want to make a fuss. I came up to bed and Frederick went back down to let the others know what had happened, otherwise I don't think they would have noticed. Edna and Horace were chatting to Gordon – the dead man – and Terry Kemble. They might be able to shed more light on things, although they both told me Gordon seemed all right apart from being a little stressed. The only thing Jasmin told me was that Gordon was the family's business accountant who wanted to speak with Oscar on a matter she shouldn't concern herself with."

"I don't suppose she, or anyone else, told you what that was?"

"As far as I can recall, Jasmin didn't know, but commented it wasn't unusual for Oscar to forget to sign important documents. She also implied Oscar wasn't always as efficient as he could be."

"Thank you, Marjorie. I've got the statement Horace made to PC Trench. If he, Edna or Frederick has anything they think I should hear, ask them to let me know. In the meantime, I'm happy for you and your friends to go to the tennis as planned, if you can face it. I have no reason to keep you here."

"That's good of you. It might be nice to get away for the day. I'll see what the others say. I'm sure Edna and Frederick will be only too pleased to get out for a bit. The other thing I should mention is that we will continue to stay here until I'm certain Jasmin is being well looked after."

"Your friend?"

"Yes."

"Is there anything in particular you're worried about? Anything you'd like to share?"

Marjorie shook her head. "Nothing I can put my finger on… just a feeling. I'll let you know if anything comes of it."

DI Bloom took out a card and scribbled on the back. "This is my mobile number. If you come up with anything or are concerned about anything, no matter how trivial, call me."

Marjorie took the card and put it in her handbag. "Thank you," she said, standing up.

"And Marjorie, I won't try telling you not to involve yourself. All I ask is that you keep me in the loop, and please be careful."

"I have no desire to involve myself in your investigation, but if we hear anything, we will let you know."

When she left, Marjorie noticed one of the men in white hovering outside the door. Had he been eavesdropping? The doors were solid. She hoped he hadn't been able to hear too much.

Chapter 15

Edna finished her breakfast and wiped crumbs from her lips with what she would describe as a posh table napkin. She had been miserable since Horace pre-warned her that the police suspected murder, and now it was confirmed. DI Bloom had ruined her day, the detective's announcement shattering any hope of the accountant's death being a suicide. No doubt Marge would want to be at the centre of yet another murder investigation.

"Come on, you two," she said, throwing the napkin on the table and pushing back her chair. "I need some air."

"Shouldn't we wait for Marjorie?" Fred asked.

"You can if you want to. I've had enough of being stuck in here with this lot." The others were congregated around the young DC and Oscar in the far corner of the room. After the initial shock, they now appeared agitated. Terry

Kemble gestured wildly while Paris Toliver stood, arms folded, foot tapping on the floor, shooting daggers at everyone. Edna wondered which one, if any of them, was the killer.

"Keep your voice down, Edna." Horace checked no-one had heard, but even the men in white weren't anywhere near them. "I'll give our names and addresses to DC Sudhik and ask Oscar to let Marjorie know we've gone for a walk. I haven't seen Johnson this morning. Does anyone know where he is?"

"He's nipped to Marge's to get her phone charger. She's apparently forgotten the bloomin' thing, again," Edna said.

"I could have lent her mine," said Fred.

"Me too," said Horace.

"And me three. Knowing Marge, it will be a ruse to send him on some covert errand, which she'll no doubt fill us in on later." Edna rolled her eyes.

Horace tapped his nose. "Ah, a bit of background research, I should think. Good idea, but how did you know where he was? You've been with me most of the time since you got up."

"I overheard Oscar telling the tall man in white to make sure Marge's chauffeur got fed, and he told him where Johnson had gone."

"Let's hope the police don't suspect he's nipped off to hide a murder weapon," said Fred. Edna gave him an incredulous look.

"That's not likely. You saw who's in charge. She's a sensible pair of hands," Horace said, lowering his voice.

"Exactly. So why are we still hanging around?" Edna complained.

"We should have that discussion when we get outside," said Fred, wiping beads of sweat from his bald head.

Horace wrote their names and addresses down on a piece of paper from a notebook he kept in his breast pocket and took it over to the DC before rejoining them.

"Come on. We've got the all-clear. I've told him where we'll be."

"Did you ask Oscar to let Marjorie know where we're heading?" Fred asked.

"I couldn't. Paris had cornered him. They seem to be locking horns about something. She's a handful; reminds me of a tsunami. Anyway, I didn't want to interrupt." Horace inclined his head to where Oscar Winchester and Paris Toliver had moved to one side and appeared to be having a heated discussion. Edna frowned.

"Yeah, I see what you mean."

"I'll ask Jamie to let her know where we've gone." With uncharacteristic confidence, Fred waltzed over to the dour bodyguard, who was not to be deterred from his mission to stay in the background and away from the detective.

"He's got more guts than I credit him for." Edna grabbed Horace's arm. "Come on, let's get out of here before Jamie sets the men in white on us."

They had got as far as the front door when Fred joined them.

"You were quick," said Horace, chuckling.

"I just hope he remembers to tell her. He seems to have a lot on his mind."

"It wouldn't surprise me if our Jamie has history with the boys in blue."

"And girls," said Edna. "You can be so sexist at times, Horace Tyler."

"It's a figure of speech, Edna. Don't take everything so literally. You know I don't have a sexist bone in my body." Horace's chortle rippled through the sombre air like a shockwave. Two CSIs in overshoes stopped mid-conversation, their eyes narrowing, their lips firm as they glared at him. After he'd stopped laughing and broke instead into a broad grin, they ignored him, returning to their hushed conversation.

"Now who needs to keep their voice down?" Edna smirked, triumphant. Even Fred sniggered before he opened the door that released them into the fresh air. Compared to the atmosphere in the house, it was blissful relief. Edna felt free again. Something about the imposing mansion and the people in it made her claustrophobic, despite its high ceilings and grand rooms. She paused to take a few deep breaths, inhaling the scent of freshly mown grass and roses. Bright sunlight lightened her mood, convincing her things couldn't be as bad as she imagined.

"What beautiful grounds. Look, there's a gate over there. I bet it leads around to the back of the house. We might get more privacy." Horace headed towards an arched metal gate.

It made sense to get away from the front. There were still a lot of police and forensics people in white coveralls carrying bags and plastic cases to and from the house. The gate was unlocked, and the latch was well-oiled so they could pass through with ease.

"I don't think this is an original feature," remarked Horace, closing the gate after them.

As they strolled along a path, the sultry morning sun beat down on their heads. Horace squinted upwards.

"It's hard to believe a murder has taken place when the sky is such a deep blue."

"If only it hadn't," said Edna.

They turned a corner and Fred whistled. "Look at this! It's like a small park."

"Granted, there are a lot of trees," Edna retorted, not in the mood for Fred to start waxing lyrical about the grounds, even if he was right. Undeterred, Fred swiped his hand across a lavender bush, releasing a flurry of scent into the air. He plucked a stem and held it to her nose.

"Lavender has calming properties, you know."

Edna inhaled the aroma and found herself almost caught up with his enthusiasm, despite her misgivings. The grounds were as grand, if not grander, than the rooms inside. As they explored, it was apparent that the grounds had been divided into segments like garden rooms, each with its own distinct character. Some were modern with sleek lines and bright colours, while others were more traditional. The grass was lush and thick, and the flowers bloomed in vibrant bursts of colour.

They took a path through a topiary garden, which led into a flower garden bursting with scent. While they walked, they didn't speak for a while, each enjoying whichever aspect of the garden most appealed to them. It was somehow cleansing after what had happened inside Hallenguard Manor.

Edna broke the silence. "You're right, Horace. If there hadn't been a murder inside that monstrous house, this would be a perfect sanctuary."

"And if a different family lived there," said Fred, laughing.

"I don't know what you've got against them, other than Oscar is brusque. He's no different from many arrogant rich men."

"Present company excepted," said Edna, smiling at Horace. For someone who could be a show-off, Horace never bragged about his wealth. His position and achievements sometimes, but never his wealth.

Fred piped up. "I agree with Edna. There's something malicious about our host, his friends and his employees. I'd be happy to leave DI Bloom to get on with the investigation. Why do you think she pretended not to know us?"

"Because, my dear Fred," said Horace, "she's astute enough to know what Marjorie is like when she sniffs trouble. The good DI may not have been delighted to hear who had found the body this morning, but she is a pragmatist and will accepts it's better to work with Marjorie – and, by association, us – than against her."

"Yeah, she learned her lesson the last time," said Edna. "But it's not just by association. All of us solve crimes, not just Marge. I don't know why she gets all the credit."

"You're a puzzle sometimes, Edna. One minute you want nothing to do with any investigating and the next you're complaining because Marjorie is the chief bloodhound and we are but a part of her pack." Horace put a comforting arm around Edna's shoulder.

"Well, I'd rather not be part of anyone's pack if you don't mind… remember, I was almost killed last time out."

"How could I forget?" Horace's eyes turned serious when he looked at her. "Then don't do anything silly."

"We're all in this together," said Fred. "If Marjorie insists on staying, we'll support her."

"You've changed your bloomin' tune. A minute ago, you were on my side."

"I still am, Edna," said Fred. "I would much rather leave. But if Marjorie stays, we all stay."

Edna opened her mouth, about to put Fred in his place for thinking he could lord it over what she and Horace did, but stopped because she knew he was right. They would stick together as a foursome. There was safety in numbers and they would be on their guard. Nothing could happen to them.

Chapter 16

"We shouldn't wander too far. Marjorie won't be able to find us," said Frederick.

As much as he was enjoying meandering through the gardens, he was worried about Marjorie. He had no reason to be, since she was quite safe in the house with all the police around, but if she came looking for them, the grounds were huge and she could get lost.

Horace and Edna were deep in conversation. Frederick understood Edna more than she knew and appreciated Horace was trying to cheer her up. Neither Frederick nor Edna had the appetite for another murder investigation, but Horace would be all gung-ho about assisting Marjorie. And the fact was, they were already involved, whether or not Frederick liked it.

Frederick sighed. He knew their paths were no longer in their control. Once Marjorie had found the body and reconnected with her old friend, Jasmin, there was no going back.

He stopped walking, calling out, "I'm going to look for Marjorie."

Horace turned around. "Do you want us to come with you?"

"No, you go on. We'll catch up with you."

Edna waved. "Watch your head don't get sunburnt."

Two days in a row, Frederick had forgotten to put on a hat. His scalp was already bright red from yesterday's outing. He'd lathered it with after-sun lotion before going to bed last night, but hadn't had time to apply sun cream after hearing the news this morning.

He hurried to take cover in the shade, cutting through a small copse where there was some welcome relief from the burning sun. As Frederick stopped for a moment to get his bearings, he heard a woman crying. The sound seemed to come from the other side of the copse.

A hand tapped him on the shoulder.

Frederick leapt into the air. Spinning around to see who his attacker was, he caught his foot in a badger's hole and fell to the ground. Pain shot through his ankle, and with his heart racing, he tried to get up.

"Are you all right? I'm sorry I startled you. It looked as though you'd seen me coming. I did wave."

The reassuring sound of Marjorie's calming voice brought peace back into Frederick's world. He put his fingers to his lips.

"Listen," he whispered. Marjorie closed her eyes and listened before indicating she, too, could hear the sobbing.

"Let's see to you first, and then we'll find out who that is. Can you stand?"

Frederick rubbed his ankle, pulled up his trouser leg and pushed down his sock to examine it.

"No harm done," he said.

"You'll have a nasty bruise on that ankle. We should get some ice on it," Marjorie said. "Are you sure it's not broken?"

Frederick wiggled his ankle around. It was sore, but mobile.

"It's fine. We'll see to it later," he said, trying to sound braver than he felt.

With a little help from Marjorie and the magic appearance of the fold-up walking stick she carried in her handbag, Frederick got to his feet. He was even more grateful for Marjorie's stick as they moved stealthily towards the source of the noise.

They arrived at a rose garden where the flowers were in full bloom, the petals a vibrant array of pink, yellow, white and red. Georgina Winchester was sitting on a bench with her head in her hands, her face pale and lined with worry.

The scent hung in the air as the two of them exchanged a glance before Marjorie approached the distraught young woman and sat down next to her. Frederick sat on the other side of her, pleased to rest his ankle.

Georgina lifted her head. Her eyes were swollen and tears poured down her face. She was beautiful, even in her current state, thought Frederick.

Marjorie spoke in a gentle voice. "Can we help you?"

Georgina dabbed at her eyes with a handkerchief and shook her head vigorously. Her lips trembled as she spoke through tearful sniffles.

"No-one can," she muttered.

"Why don't you take some deep breaths and tell us what has upset you so?"

"Haven't you heard? My lover is dead," Georgina squealed, shoulders heaving as she went into another sobbing fit.

If Marjorie was taken aback, she didn't show it. Frederick was pleased he hadn't been alone. He wouldn't have known what to say.

"You and Gordon Collins were lovers," Marjorie said calmly. "I'm so sorry for your loss."

"Are you shocked?" Georgina wiped tears away, staring at Marjorie. Frederick noticed the spark of determination in her eyes that had replaced the earlier despair.

"I've lived far too long to be shocked by most things," said Marjorie. "Does your husband know about the affair?"

Panic filled Georgina's eyes. "No. He must never know. I don't know what he'd do if he found out. He's a jealous man."

Or what he might already have done, thought Frederick.

"He won't hear anything from us, my dear. Unless, of course…" Marjorie didn't finish that sentence, moving on instead. "Did anyone else know about your affair?"

Georgina shook her head again. "Not as far as I'm aware. I think Gordon was getting impatient, though."

"What do you mean?" Marjorie asked.

"We talked about my leaving Oscar and us running away together…" Georgina mock laughed, opening her hands palms up. "It was an impossible dream."

"Is that because you're frightened of your husband?" Marjorie prompted.

"Not just Oscar. Everyone who works for him. Living in that house is suffocating."

"Are you absolutely certain he didn't suspect you were lovers?" Frederick asked.

Georgina blew her nose. "If he had, he would have mentioned it." She spat the words out with such venom Frederick's eyes popped. "My husband is evil. Those who work for him are evil. Gordon was so tender – the complete opposite to Oscar. That's why I was falling in love with him."

"Then why didn't you leave your husband?" Marjorie asked.

"Because it was a stupid idea. I'm addicted to the lifestyle, the wealth and all that goes with it. How could I give all this up to run away with an accountant? Besides, I don't think Gordon would have gone through with it."

Frederick's sympathy was evaporating by the minute, but Marjorie wasn't showing any signs of the judgement he felt.

"Did Gordon threaten to tell your husband?"

Frederick's ears pricked up. *Of course! That's why Gordon was at the house last night. Maybe the business he had to discuss was personal.*

"No. Gordon had a pipe dream we would one day be together, but that's all it was – a dream. He was practical enough to realise that Oscar's business was too important to him. His father had built up the firm, but Oscar's was the only business Gordon worked on – it's… was… a full-time job. He was almost an employee for the lack of control he had. My husband likes to be in control of everything."

There was that bitter tone again. Why would a woman who practically hated her husband and said she loved another man stay in a marriage for money? It wasn't something Frederick could get his head around.

"I'm sorry to keep asking you this, but you're quite certain neither your husband nor any of his employees knew about Gordon?" Marjorie pressed.

"As sure as I can be. We only ever met off premises, in hotels on the outskirts of London. We had planned to meet yesterday until you arrived and Oscar changed his mind about working. If I'm honest, Oscar has been distracted of late, and we took advantage of it, fitting in time when we could. I've been sleeping in my own room and have not had to fight about it for weeks."

"Can you remember anything triggering this change in Oscar's behaviour?" Marjorie asked.

Georgina dabbed at her eyes once more. At least the crying had stopped.

"Most likely something to do with the hotels. I pay little attention to his business affairs."

You just spend the money, thought Frederick, shocked at how judgemental he was being. It's not as if Oscar deserved his sympathy.

"Back to your question about anyone knowing. If anyone would have sussed it out, it would have been Slimy Jamie Peeble. He watches everyone like a master vulture, looking for any sign of weakness. I'm pretty sure he's got something over on most of the staff – maybe even Oscar himself. I don't know why my husband still employs him. Peeble pretends to be subservient, but he's downright insubordinate."

"In what way?" Frederick asked.

"That gun he carries for one. Oscar has told him time after time to lock it away, but he takes no notice. What he doesn't know is that Oscar switched his bullets to blanks and keeps the real ones under lock and key."

"Oscar said as much when Edna challenged him about the gun over breakfast while Jamie was out of the room," Marjorie said. "If Jamie had known about your affair, what do you think he would have done with the information?"

"I guess he would have tried to extort money, or influence Gordon in some way."

"Why not you?" Frederick asked.

"Because Oscar would have found out. What I spend is monitored, although my husband is not ungenerous on that front. He would have noticed if large sums of cash were withdrawn."

"You don't think he would have told Oscar about the affair?" Marjorie asked.

"As I said, if he had, Oscar would have told me to end it. Look, I'd better get back to the house now or he'll wonder where I am. I don't know how I'm going to get through this."

My heart bleeds, thought Frederick cynically.

Georgina hesitated. "Do you think Jamie could have been blackmailing Gordon? Is that why he killed himself? It would be a relief if that was the reason, because I've been blaming myself. If we had only managed some time together yesterday, he could have told me what was troubling him. I could have dealt with Jamie somehow and we might have carried on the way we were."

"I'm sorry to be the one to tell you," said Marjorie, "but the police believe Gordon was murdered."

Georgina blinked several times, the colour draining from her face. "No. That's not possible. Is that why you've been asking all these questions? You believe Oscar killed Gordon, don't you?" Disbelief turned to fear, then anger. Georgina shook Marjorie's hand away, got up and stumbled through the garden back towards the house.

"Should we go after her?" Frederick asked.

Marjorie shook her head, deep in thought, before asking, "How's the ankle?"

Chapter 17

Marjorie and Frederick had remained on the bench after Georgina left. Each was lost in their own thoughts. Frederick's eyes were fixed on a point in the distance, while Marjorie watched with interest as a pair of robins flitted back and forth to a nest tucked in a nearby hedge, not far off the ground. She couldn't help thinking how much simpler life could be if humans didn't complicate things.

Their tranquil moment was shattered when she heard two familiar voices heading their way. Horace and Edna appeared in view.

Edna exclaimed, hands on hips, "Ah-ha! There you are, Marge. We've been looking everywhere for you, and you're lounging on a bench. Bloomin' typical."

"Don't exaggerate, Edna," said Horace. "We've enjoyed a lovely stroll. My goodness, what's wrong with your ankle, Fred?"

Frederick had rolled up his trouser leg again to let the air get to the purpling bruise. He answered calmly, although it was obvious to Marjorie that it was sore.

"I tripped over."

Horace gave him a look of sympathy. "You've got quite a bruise there."

Marjorie would have explained how she had startled the poor man, except she knew Edna would tease him without mercy and call him a wuss or some such name, so she changed tack.

"We've just had an interesting conversation with Georgina Winchester."

"Oh? What about?" Horace asked.

Marjorie looked around. The gardens appeared quiet, but there were far too many places for someone to be lurking.

She made her decision. "If Frederick's up to it, I suggest we leave Hallenguard—"

"Thank the Lord!" Edna exclaimed.

"That we leave the house *for a while*." Edna's face dropped. "DI Bloom – I take it you remember her?"

"How could we forget," said Edna, "you and Mr Universe here crossing her crime scene?"

Horace chuckled, mock flexing his muscles.

"Oh, do be serious." Marjorie couldn't hide a grin herself. "As I was saying, DI Bloom is happy for now with the statement Horace gave to PC Trench, although she said to contact her if you wanted to tell her anything else. But as we are not under suspicion, we can go to the tennis."

"Oh, goody," said Edna, frowning.

"It's better than staying here," Frederick said. "I'm sure my ankle will hold up. It's just a bruise."

"It's getting near lunchtime, Edna," said Horace. "We can either stay here for another bring in or we could have a hearty lunch at Wimbledon."

"You're on," said Edna.

"That's settled, then. I agree it's not ideal. At first, I dismissed the idea in my head, but it will do us good to get away while the police carry out their interviews," said Marjorie. "Once we've found Johnson, we can tell you what we found out from Georgina."

"Is it too much to hope that DI Bloom will have the crime solved by the time we get back?" Frederick gave a hopeful smile.

"Who knows?" said Horace, forever the optimist. "She might well have done."

The four headed back towards the house with a sense of purpose. They found a row of rhododendrons and hovered there while Marjorie checked her phone. Johnson had texted to say he was on the way back.

"What about Jasmin?" Frederick asked. "Are you happy to leave her?"

Marjorie wondered again whether she was right to involve her friends in something that was none of their business. It's not as if they had known Gordon Collins.

"You understand, I have to find out what's going on, for Jasmin's sake? For now, David will give her all the support she needs."

Marjorie recognised the faraway look in Frederick's eye. Memories of intimacy were all they had left of their late spouses.

"He's in love with her, isn't he?"

"It seems that way—"

"I don't suppose you ever found out what it was Oscar wanted to talk to you about, Marge?" Edna interrupted, sidling up to Marjorie.

"We haven't had the time to talk, really, and as he stood us up yesterday, he might have changed his mind. He's made no effort to mention it again."

"I bet he didn't apologise for standing us up, either."

"You're quite right. Oscar doesn't strike me as the apologising type. I wish Johnson would hurry. We're starting to draw attention."

One of the men in white stood on the top step, looking their way. At first, he'd been watching the comings and goings of the forensic team, but now they were packing up, there was only Marjorie and her friends to look at.

Edna sniffed at a large rhododendron, pretending to point to it whilst speaking in a hushed tone. "Why do they feel the need to spy on us in particular?"

"Perhaps they're frightened we'll run away with the antiquities." Marjorie remembered Edna's faux pas when they'd arrived yesterday and wondered if Jamie had mentioned it to the men in white.

"Not funny, Marge."

"Here's Johnson now," said Horace.

"Good. Let's go," said Frederick.

They waited for Johnson to park before heading his way. Marjorie's loyal chauffeur and friend got out of the Rolls.

"Sorry it took me so long. The traffic was dreadful coming into Wimbledon. I guess it's the tennis."

"Did you manage to get anything to eat?" Marjorie asked.

"Yes, thanks. Gloria rustled me up some kippers while I rang around."

"We'll discuss the phoning round in the car. The police have given us a reprieve to go to the tennis and we're taking it. I'll just let the good man in white know where we're going." Marjorie climbed the steps, thankful there was no sign of the taller, more austere man. "Please, could you let Mr Winchester know we will be out for the rest of the day? The inspector has given us permission to leave."

The man spluttered a little, but Marjorie didn't give him time to speak. The others were already in the car and Johnson was holding the door open. Then he waved at the stocky man.

"See you later, mate."

Before long, they were stuck in slow traffic heading to the All England Tennis Club.

"I feel like a naughty schoolboy skiving off school," said Frederick.

"You never did?" Edna teased, happily chatting now that they were away from Hallenguard Manor. There followed a bit of banter between Frederick and Edna, which helped them all to unwind while they stayed off topic for a few minutes.

Once the hubbub died down, Marjorie asked, "So, Johnson, did you uncover anything useful?"

"I hope you don't mind, but I used the house phone once I found the address book where you said it would be. I called all the people on your list."

"Of course I don't mind. You asked them for complete discretion, I hope?" Marjorie had given Johnson a list of her closest confidantes. There were some that would be prone to gossip, so she had asked him to avoid calling them.

Johnson glanced in the rear-view mirror. "Don't worry. They said they'd be only too happy to help, and they sent their regards. None of them could give me any useful information, but they promised to look into it and get back to me if they find out anything."

Marjorie couldn't help feeling disappointed, even though she'd suspected the calls would be unlikely to yield any breakthrough news.

"At least that's something. The DI in charge of the investigation is someone we met in the Highlands last year. She doesn't suspect any of us of being involved, so if you would rather go home later, you are quite welcome to."

Johnson hesitated. "If it's all the same to you, Marjorie, I'd like to stay."

"Are you sure, Johnson?"

"I might be able to find out something useful below stairs, if you know what I mean."

"Okay, Johnson. See what you can discover, but do be careful. Someone in that house is a killer and until we know who that is, we can't rule anyone out, including the staff."

"Don't worry about me, I grew up in the East End. It was tough, but you learned how to watch your back. It's them upstairs you need to worry about – wolves in sheep's clothing and all that."

Marjorie had always known Johnson was intelligent and sensible. He had been a good friend to Ralph when he was alive and to her since his passing. Johnson could be trusted, and if there was anything to find out from Oscar's employees, he would discover it.

"We'll *all* be careful."

"Righto," he said. "I've already discovered John and Vic like a drink before they go to bed, and I reckon I can get them talking. They've opened up a bit. Even if they don't, Alison and Kris like to talk."

Marjorie hadn't considered how useful employees could be when it came to uncovering information on families like the Winchesters.

"Who are these people?"

"John's the big fella in the white or grey uniform and Vic's the little, stocky guy you spoke to when we were leaving just now."

"So, the men in white have names? That's good to know. It makes them less intimidating."

"They're all right. I don't think either of them like the job, but the pay's good."

"What is their job, exactly?" Frederick asked.

"Gofers. They do whatever is needed. Serve dinners, look after guests – that kind of thing. Boring stuff mostly."

"Why do they have to be so surly?" Marjorie asked.

"Are they?" Johnson laughed. "I can ask when I get to know them better if it's part of the job description."

"And who are Alison and Kris?" Frederick asked.

"I only met them briefly yesterday, but they nattered nonstop about the family. Kris is the chef, and Alison manages the house. I think there are others, but I haven't met them yet."

"Oscar mentioned the Alison woman at breakfast, Marge. She's the one that owns the black cat," said Edna.

"So he did," Marjorie answered. "And Paris put her down, if my memory serves me right."

"Yeah, she's as volatile as Oscar is. Can you imagine them two being married?"

Horace snorted with laughter. "It would be pistols at dawn every morning."

"Johnson, would you mind stopping at that chemist, please?" Marjorie had noticed Frederick wincing. Johnson stopped the car. "We could get you an ankle support and some anti-inflammatory cream," she said.

"Good idea. Come on, Fred," said Horace.

When the two men returned, Frederick looked a lot more comfortable.

"Do you mind if I drop you at the gate and disappear for a bit? I don't think I fancy queueing today," Johnson said.

Marjorie knew there would be a lengthy queue today. "It's ladies' quarter-finals day, so it can be rather busy. We'll give you a ring about an hour before we're ready to leave, or we could get a taxi?"

"No, I'll be on hand. I've got a cousin just up the road in Wandsworth. She gets lonely, so I said I'd try to pop in sometime this week."

"Thank you, Johnson. We'll fill you in on what we discovered this morning when we see you this evening."

Johnson drove into Church Road and pulled up outside Gate 4, where there was a much smaller queue of debenture ticket holders. He got out and opened the rear doors.

Edna climbed out. "It makes me feel like royalty whenever I travel with you, Johnson." She straightened the purple wig. "Wish I'd worn a different colour now," she said.

Me too, thought Marjorie.

Chapter 18

The buzz around the tennis grounds was infectious from the moment they stepped inside. Horace guided them upstairs to the Courtside Restaurant on level three of the Centre Court debenture lounge complex.

A waiter took Horace's name and showed them to the same table they had sat around the day before. Marjorie looked out of a window overlooking two other courts where some doubles matches were taking place.

"How come we get shown to the same table every time we come here?" Edna asked.

"Because I pre-booked," Horace explained. "I guessed what time we'd be eating and booked accordingly. So far, it's worked out well."

"No wonder you said when we should go eat last night," Edna said, grinning.

The restaurant was busy, but orderly, like everything they had witnessed so far at the Championships. It was in stark contrast to the goings on at Hallenguard Manor.

"Are you saying these tables have to be booked?" Marjorie asked.

"Yes," Horace replied.

"So how could Oscar have joined us last night had he turned up?"

"That's a good question, Marjorie. I suppose he would have dragged us off to another one where booking isn't required."

"It makes you wonder whether he ever had any intention of coming at all yesterday," said Frederick.

Marjorie had just been wondering the same thing. "But why would he do that?"

"To upset his wife," said Edna. "He was relishing her reaction."

"Speaking of which," said Horace, "let's order lunch, and then you can tell us what you and Fred found out from Georgina."

Edna and Horace ordered three course lunches, but Marjorie could only face a main wanting to save herself for strawberries and cream later on. Frederick opted for two courses. When the waiter offered to bring champagne, Edna's hand went to her head.

"I think I'll settle for mineral water today."

The rest of them also requested soft drinks, Marjorie because she wanted to keep her wits about her rather than from over-indulging the day before.

Once starters were served to her three friends, Marjorie told them about her and Frederick hearing Georgina weeping in the rose garden after Frederick had injured his ankle.

"How is it now?" she asked.

"Much better with the support, thank you."

Edna couldn't resist an eye roll, but said nothing rude.

Marjorie carried on with the story, explaining what Georgina had told them about her affair with Gordon.

"Oscar didn't come off well from what she told us. She seemed to be frightened of him and I'm sorry to say she gave the impression of hating him, if that's not too strong a word. And yet, she didn't want to leave him, or rather, leave the life she had become used to."

Edna frowned. "I'd leave him in a heartbeat. Lording it over everyone like he's some sort of ancient baron. No amount of money is worth being that miserable."

Horace looked thoughtful. "Perhaps the misery is more to do with her boyfriend being murdered. Maybe she is content with her lot, and her lover fulfilled the other side of life that she needed, if you know what I mean?"

"Don't be vulgar, Horace Tyler. It don't suit you," said Edna. "Couldn't lover-boy have given her a decent lifestyle?"

"Not according to her," said Frederick. "Apparently, Gordon had all his eggs in the one company... Oscar's. It would have been hard for him to go it alone. Besides, I suspect she'd have soon got bored if the affair became a proper relationship. Women like that always do."

"Get you, Mr *I don't like women having affairs*, but probably don't mind when men do," said Edna.

"That's not what Frederick meant," said Marjorie. "But when pressed, Georgina wondered whether Jamie knew about their assignations. She suggested he wouldn't have been shy about resorting to blackmail rather than tell her husband."

"She hates Jamie almost as much as she does Oscar," Frederick added.

"Hmm." Horace stroked his chin. "But if Oscar had found out, would he have been angry enough to kill his accountant?"

"That's the other thing. Georgina believed Gordon had killed himself. She was distraught and terrified when we told her the police believed he had been murdered."

"Do you think she was being genuine?" Horace quizzed.

"Her reaction suggested she was," said Frederick.

"So, the question remains: did Oscar find out about the affair? If so, case closed. He's our killer."

Marjorie had been mulling that question over in her head, knowing DI Bloom was likely to come to the same conclusion once she found out about the affair. And Marjorie knew the inspector would find out.

"I suggest we park Oscar as a suspect for now. Something else Georgina mentioned was that he had been distracted in recent weeks, which she put down to business worries. Could that be what he wanted to speak to me about yesterday?"

"But if so, why didn't he turn up?" said Edna.

Marjorie raised an eyebrow. "I don't know. Pride? He might have found it too much to confide in a woman when it came down to it."

"Some men would find that sort of thing hard, but if he'd invited you to stay for the sole purpose of sharing whatever it was with you, why go back on it?" Horace said.

"It's one reason I asked Johnson to look into Oscar's businesses. I thought it might at least give us a clue what it was Gordon wanted to speak to him about. That was before I knew about the affair."

"Hence the phone charger fiasco," said Edna. "We heard all about that."

"Ah, yes. Well, it was the first thing that came to mind. Quite plausible that a forgetful elderly aristocrat might forget to bring a charger with her."

"When most of her friends have the same phone," said Edna.

"I doubt anyone would notice," Marjorie countered.

"Don't you believe it, Marge. Those men in white have eyes everywhere."

"You mean Vic and John?"

"Thank heavens we managed to get away from the house for a while," said Frederick.

"You don't think it's bugged, do you?" Edna asked, her eyes wide with horror. "Or that they have cameras in our rooms?" Her hands automatically went to her wig.

"We're letting our imaginations run wild again," said Horace.

Marjorie shook her head. "Until proven otherwise, we are staying at the home of a perfectly respectable man."

"Who could be a murderer," Edna said, sullenly.

"Where there's a murderer on the loose," Horace acknowledged. "Oscar might not be to our taste, but I can't believe he would kill a man over an affair with his wife."

Frederick cleared his throat. "Men have killed for less."

"Not men like Oscar Winchester. He's more pragmatic," said Horace.

"Oh, you know him well, do you?" Edna challenged.

"Arguing amongst ourselves will not get us anywhere," said Marjorie after the first course plates had been cleared away and their mains were served. "We will not forget that Oscar could have a powerful motive for murder if he knew his wife was having an affair, but for now, we have no evidence to suggest he did it."

"The gun-wielding Jamie might have," said Edna.

"He doesn't have a motive for murder," Horace said.

"What if Gordon refused to pay up and Jamie lost his rag? You've seen the size of him and, let's face it, he would be strong enough to hang the man to death."

"DI Bloom told me the pathologist believes someone strangled Gordon, and the hanging was used to cover up the first crime," Marjorie said.

"We can't rule Georgina out either. Her tears may have been more to do with remorse than loss," Frederick added.

"Surely a woman—"

"Don't finish that sentence, Horace Tyler," Edna warned. "I've heard enough sexist remarks from you for one day."

Marjorie sympathised with Horace. He liked to believe women were incapable of murder, but real life showed the opposite. On this occasion, she agreed with him, though. Strangling wasn't usually a woman's murder method. She decided not to mention that just now for fear of riling Edna.

"We need to do a little more digging into this family and Gordon Collins. There might be other secrets he's taken with him. Secrets someone was willing to kill for. I wonder if we could get inside Oscar's study. There might be something in there that would give us a hint."

Edna scowled. "Not with Jamie around. No way, Marge… too dangerous."

"Could Gordon have been swindling money out of Oscar's business?" Frederick asked. "Another thing that would implicate Oscar in his murder."

"You appeared to be getting on well with him and Terry last night. Did he give you any clue why he wanted to speak to Oscar?" Marjorie asked Edna.

She shook her head. "Nope, he didn't say much at all. Terry was the one who did all the talking. He was like a hare on speed."

Horace chortled, snorting at the same time, which broke the atmosphere. Edna joined in. Marjorie, although chuckling at the imagery, and Frederick waited for the joint snorts to end, thankful that the restaurant was noisy enough for people not to pay them much attention.

"I wonder if the answer lies in Gordon's briefcase," said Marjorie.

"I didn't see him carrying one, but I'm sure Patricia Bloom will be thorough. Are you sure you want to stay there, Marge? Wouldn't you rather find a hotel and carry on with our tennis break from there? Fred wants to leave, don't you?"

"Do you?" Marjorie felt guilty about Frederick's ankle and the stress he and Edna would go through due to her desire to solve another murder, but she'd already made it clear she owed it to Jasmin, and possibly even Gordon Collins, to find out what was going on.

Frederick closed his eyes briefly. "Perhaps we could help the police a little while still doing what we came to do."

Marjorie knew what it cost him to say what he did, which made her even more grateful. She gave him a warm smile of thanks for understanding her desire to solve the mystery, whatever the consequences.

"The sooner we get started, the sooner we move on," said Horace cheerfully. "How about it, Edna?"

Edna nodded reluctantly. "Save me from bloomin' amateur detectives. Let's get on with the tennis first."

"Your burgeoning passion for tennis is astounding," said Marjorie. Loud guffaws from Frederick and Horace followed, and even Edna forced a smile.

"Hilarious, Marge."

Chapter 19

Jasmin was in the main hall, shooing David away while she spoke to the tall man Marjorie now knew was called John. For the first time, Marjorie saw him grin. It was obvious from the brief encounter he liked Jasmin.

"Marjorie, Frederick, how good to see you both. Your friends are having breakfast in the dining room." With a nod from Jasmin, John disappeared down the stairs to the kitchen.

"How are you feeling?" Marjorie asked as she was pulled in for two air kisses.

"A lot better for seeing you." David hovered in the background, making Marjorie feel uncomfortable. His dedication, however sweet, was overbearing.

"I see the police have removed the cordon," Frederick said. Marjorie had noticed it gone last night when she and her friends sneaked in via the kitchen, but hadn't wanted to mention it then.

"Only to allow access into the kitchen. There's one at the foot of the stairs, which Casper doesn't like. He seems to have taken a shine to your friend Horace. He wouldn't leave him alone, although I'm not so sure Edna is a fan of my feline companion."

Marjorie smiled. "She got on very well with a dog who was staying with us over Christmas, but don't tell her I said that because she'll deny it."

"I'm so pleased you managed to get out yesterday. Did you enjoy the tennis?"

"We did, thank you. Sorry for leaving you like that, but with the place swarming with police, once we were given the all-clear, we thought it best to leave them to their work. We're giving the tennis a miss today, though, if you don't mind us being here?"

"Not at all. I'd be delighted."

Marjorie used her eyes to motion to Frederick to get David away from them. He understood and did so with aplomb.

"We'll have time to catch up at last," said Marjorie when the two men had walked away, talking.

"Oh good. Kris, our chef, has prepared breakfast for you in the dining room – I ate with Oscar and Georgina before they left – and he'll be preparing a light lunch later.

As we missed out on our breakfast yesterday, I'd love it if you and your friends would join me for lunch. Oscar's gone to one of his hotels and Terry's left for a meeting. Paris has taken Georgina shopping to cheer her up, so it's just us in the house today."

"I'm sure we'd love to, thank you," said Marjorie. "What about Jamie and David?"

"Jamie goes where Oscar goes and David's got a round of golf booked. He offered to cancel, but I wouldn't hear of it. Life must go on." Jasmin sighed, although on the whole she was back to being the cheerful, outgoing woman Marjorie had previously known. The one she had seen glimpses of on their first night.

"I'll let Horace and Edna know. Did you say they were already in the dining room?"

"Yes, with Casper. If he's being a nuisance, ask Vic or John to put him out, will you?"

"And the police?"

A flicker of a frown crossed Jasmin's face. "Inspector Bloom said she would be back later. I don't know what else she thinks we can tell her. I'm sure it was suicide. Nobody here would want to kill anyone."

"Don't trouble yourself thinking about it." David appeared at Jasmin's side once more. Frederick gave Marjorie an apologetic glance.

"Well, I'll let you get on with your breakfast," said Jasmin. "Would you join me for lunch on my patio?"

"I'll look forward to it," said Marjorie.

"Wonderful. If noon suits, I'll see you there?"

"Noon sounds perfect," said Marjorie.

She and Frederick left David to cluck around Jasmin while they retraced their steps to the dining room they had eaten in the day before.

"Thank you for helping there. I realise he cares about her, but he's almost suffocating," Marjorie said.

"I expect he's overcompensating because of the death in the house. He does seem overprotective."

"Jasmin's invited us all for lunch on her patio, and the kitchen's open again," said Marjorie, winking.

"Funnily enough, I noticed last night. I was surprised when nobody accosted us on the way up the stairs. Thanks to our day away, I slept better last night."

Marjorie chuckled. "Me too, especially after taking a glass of water to bed with me and locking the door."

They had been delighted to return to a quiet house with no-one demanding they were elsewhere. Oscar's limousine had been on the drive, but there wasn't a light on when they got back. Horace had joked that the entire household had been murdered, but stopped when Edna refused to go a step further until he had checked the coast was clear.

Frederick was walking better this morning. Marjorie had been concerned he might find the ankle had swelled overnight, but he had assured her when they met on the landing that it was the opposite.

"Let's get some breakfast and tell Horace and Edna about lunch," she said. "Did David have anything interesting to say?"

"Just that the police had left at around eight last night and Terry got to go to his meeting, and another one today, and Paris had stomped around all day complaining about being kept prisoner."

"Anything about Oscar?"

Frederick shook his head. "Other than after his interview, he locked himself away in his office for most of the day, and that he and Georgina hardly spoke. David thought they'd had a row."

"That's quite a bit of information you gleaned in a brief space of time," said Marjorie.

"We seemed to hit it off. He's not so stuck up as Oscar and Paris."

"Precisely."

Edna and Horace were finishing their breakfast when they entered. Marjorie heard Casper purring and was horrified to see the animal sitting on Horace's lap while he ate.

Horace noticed. "Whoops. Caught in the act. You'd better go down, boy." He placed the disgruntled animal on the floor.

"Good morning, Casper," Marjorie said as the cat stalked haughtily from the room.

"I swear cats communicate better than dogs," said Horace.

"In which case we should ask Ben who killed Gordon because he's our only witness," Marjorie said.

"What are you talking about, Marge? Who's Ben?"

"The house manager's cat," said Horace. "As Oscar told us just yesterday morning."

Edna harrumphed.

"Good morning to you too, Edna," said Marjorie.

"Hello, Marge. I don't mind us staying here today now I know most of 'em are out. Apart from David and your mate, that is."

Surprised he was honoured with his full name rather than a diminutive, Marjorie said, "David's about to leave for a round of golf. Jasmin invited us for lunch at noon."

"I can live with that," said Edna. "It means I might get a nap in the garden. There's a lovely water fountain visible from my room. I thought I'd go and explore."

"Did Jasmin say anything about the police investigation? We didn't like to ask," said Horace.

"Just that DI Bloom is coming back sometime today. David told Frederick they packed up around eight last night."

"She's been and gone," said Edna, rolling her eyes.

"Really? Did you find anything out?" Marjorie asked, checking the door to make sure there was no sign of John or Vic.

"Hey, Marge, DI Bloom was interviewing us, not the other way round." Edna cackled. "And I'm warning you, she might act like she's your best mate, but she ain't forgot you're an interfering busybody."

Marjorie grinned, remembering how Patricia Bloom had warned her and her friends off during the previous investigation before having to accept their help. "The inspector is intelligent enough to let us do a little sleuthing and help her with her enquiries," she said, chuckling. "What did she say other than that I'm an interfering busybody?"

"That's not what she said at all," said Horace. "She was far more tactful. The inspector suggested we make sure you know your limitations."

Marjorie giggled.

"As if—" Edna puffed.

"The police don't know about the affair yet," Horace interrupted. "Or if they do, they didn't mention it. I got the impression they're looking for a financial motive rather than a grudge. Not that they've ruled anything out – even a random intruder."

"The financial motive makes sense, bearing in mind Gordon's job. It's something we should consider. I don't know whether I told you this, but my family's business had a dodgy accountant once." Marjorie shuddered. "But that brings back memories I'd rather forget."

"I hate it when people tell you half a story – or in this case, a fraction of a story," Edna moaned.

"Accountants can make or break a business if they're heavily involved," said Horace. "We've had the same firm at Tyler Avionics ever since I started out, but I've had friends who've had dirty ones. We need to find out whether Gordon Collins was clean or dirty."

"Precisely," said Marjorie. "If he was clean, he may have uncovered something important enough to interrupt Oscar at home, and if he was a crook, it may have got him killed."

"There's still the affair angle to consider," said Frederick. "Why didn't you tell DI Bloom about that?"

"We thought we'd leave the snitching to you," snapped Edna.

"Unless it's relevant to the investigation, I'm not sure we should mention it," Marjorie said. "I promised Georgina I wouldn't tell Oscar."

"But that's up to the inspector to decide, isn't it?" Frederick argued. "How can she do her job if she doesn't have all the information? It's not like you would be telling Oscar."

"It's as good as telling him," said Marjorie.

"Fred's right, you know," said Horace. "If Georgina hasn't told the inspector, someone has to."

"I'll try to have a word with Georgina," said Marjorie. "It would be better coming from her, but you know it will put Oscar in the frame for murder."

"Frankly," said Horace, "he's got at least one motive, possibly two if Gordon was crooked. And the means – he admitted his wife slept in a separate room the night of the murder. He could have arranged to meet Gordon after everyone had gone to bed, knocked him off and made the murder look like a suicide. Who else would know there was a Victorian laundry hanger in the scullery?"

"Yeah, right," said Edna.

"There's still the Jamie angle," said Marjorie. "He might have found out about the affair."

"What about Georgina herself?" said Frederick. "What if Gordon decided he'd had enough of playing lover and wanted more, so he threatened to tell Oscar about the affair, and that's the reason he was here the night before last?"

Marjorie felt a headache coming on. "It's clear there's still a lot of ground to go over, but you are all right. The inspector needs to know about the affair."

"Not half," said Edna.

"I've got her phone number in my handbag. She gave it to me yesterday," said Marjorie.

"Well, don't go ringing her now because she got called to the morgue."

Marjorie felt relieved. She might get time to speak to Georgina when she returned from her shopping trip.

"Right now, I'm going for a walk. You coming?" Edna nudged Horace. It seemed to be more of a demand than a request.

After Horace and Edna left, Marjorie felt out of sorts. Perhaps she should call Inspector Bloom right away, whatever she was doing, and tell her about the affair. The murder could be a simple case of jealous rage. But what if it was something more sinister? Marjorie had to find out.

Chapter 20

At noon, the four friends made their way to Jasmin's private apartment, led by Marjorie, who tapped on the open door.

"Out here," Jasmin called. "Come on through."

When they joined Jasmin outside, Marjorie looked around. A terracotta-painted stone wall neatly arranged and enclosed the modern paving and manicured borders, giving the area a Mediterranean feel. The sun lit up the patio and the vibrant colours of the flowers created a rainbow palette.

"Please sit down," said Jasmin.

They sat with Marjorie's friend at the freshly laid wooden dining table, covered by a retractable awning matching the walls. The men in white approached from an outside path carrying two large, generously loaded food trays, which they set down.

"Thank you, John. Thank you, Vic," Jasmin said.

"I'll just get some fresh juice and we'll bring tea after you've eaten," said John.

"I see your new best mate's here, Horace," said Edna.

Marjorie turned her head to see Casper sprawled out in a sunny spot with a bowl of water nearby.

"Casper loves it out here," said Jasmin.

"Yeah, seems even Horace's charm can't beat a catnap," said Edna.

Horace smiled. "I'm still finding cat hair on my trousers, so he's fine where he is."

Moments later, Vic came back and set two pitchers of drink on the table, along with empty glasses. "Fresh orange juice from the orangery on site and elderflower cordial," he said.

"I didn't realise you had an orangery," said Marjorie after Vic had left them to eat.

"We have a team of gardeners who take care of the grounds, so we grow most of our own fruit and vegetables. It was something Hugh insisted upon. If he'd had the time, I'm sure we would have kept livestock too." Jasmin smiled, a faraway look in her eyes.

After the initial conversation, Jasmin appeared frail throughout their lunch, hardly speaking and picking at her food. Marjorie wondered if she had a problem with blood sugar and poured her a generous glass of orange juice.

"Here, my dear. Drink this. It will give you energy."

"Thank you," but Jasmin's eyes had glazed over.

"It's beautiful out here," said Horace. "A lovely bit of privacy for you in such a large house."

"I find it peaceful," said Jasmin, blinking her eyes, clearly trying to refocus.

"Is something troubling you?" Marjorie asked.

Jasmin put a hand to her head. "Things seem awfully fuzzy sometimes."

"You've had an eventful few days," said Horace. "My head's spinning with it all, too. Would you rather we leave you to get some rest?"

"No. Please don't go. I feel... I don't know how to explain it... safe... ever since the four of you arrived. It's—"

"Mother! What are you doing out here in this heat? You know you should be resting." Oscar had appeared out of nowhere with a sullen Vic at his rear. His tone was like a whip cracking through the surroundings.

"It's just lunch," said Horace, looking as surprised as Marjorie was by Oscar's outburst. Marjorie could have hugged him, and she didn't miss the hint of a grin from Vic.

"She has to rest!" shouted Oscar, his neck veins bulging.

"Chill, Oscar!" Edna exclaimed. "We'll finish our lunch and make sure your mother's tucked up afterwards. She's just enjoying a catch up with her old friend."

Jasmin shook herself, suddenly lucid. "Yes, I am, Oscar. Please leave us now." Her voice was firm and unyielding.

Oscar's jaw tightened. "If you wish." Turning to Vic, he snarled, "You make sure she gets some rest afterwards."

"Yes, sir," the man answered, looking triumphant.

As soon as Oscar left, John appeared with a tea tray. He and Vic poured tea until John sidled up to Edna.

"Yours is coffee, I believe?" It was the first hint of warmth towards her friends Marjorie had seen from the sullen man.

"Ooh, ta. I do prefer coffee to tea." Edna smiled at John.

The men cleared away the lunch trays and dishes, leaving the friends with side plates and a selection of cakes and scones.

"Take your time, Mrs Winchester," Vic said, flashing a caring smile.

"Yes. You enjoy time with your friends," said John.

The two men left, grinning and nudging each other. It was the happiest they had been since Marjorie and her friends had arrived.

"Was my son here a moment ago?" Jasmin asked.

"Yes, he was," said Marjorie, concerned again.

"He takes good care of me since his father died. He's very attentive."

Too attentive, if you ask me, thought Marjorie, but said nothing.

"Do you have children?" Jasmin asked Horace, who was helping himself to a slice of lemon drizzle cake.

"Two sons," he said, "and five grandchildren. They're all grown up now. I was explaining to the others when we arrived how convenient it was your son inviting us to stay here because the grandkids have descended on my London flat for the week."

"I have a son and a daughter," said Frederick, "and four grandchildren."

"It must be nice to have grandchildren," Jasmin said. "Oscar and Georgina don't seem to… well… they don't seem to want children."

"I couldn't have kids. It's not a given that everyone produces offspring." Edna sounded matter of fact, but Marjorie knew her cousin-in-law had longed for children in her younger days.

"That could be it," said Jasmin. "Perhaps Georgina can't have children."

Marjorie ignored Jasmin's assumption it was Georgina's problem because she wanted to take advantage of her friend's flashes of lucidness. She wasn't sure, though, how to bring the conversation around to Gordon Collins.

Frederick came to the rescue. "Do you know whether Gordon had children?"

It worked. Jasmin thought for a moment. "You know, I don't know as much as I should about him, considering he was our accountant. I knew his father better, but I know Gordon is… was married and had two girls. I hope someone told them. Poor children, to lose their father at such a young age."

Frederick scowled into his tea. Marjorie knew he would be fuming at the fact Gordon had been unfaithful to his wife and family.

"I'm surprised he didn't wear a wedding ring," Edna remarked. Marjorie was surprised, too, but for other reasons. How could Gordon have been contemplating starting a new life with Georgina? No wonder Georgina had said it was a flight of fantasy and wouldn't happen.

"Not all men wear wedding rings," Jasmin said. "But I met his wife last year. They came to one of Oscar's entertainment dos. A pleasant woman, I recall. She showed me a photograph of their girls. Eight and ten, I think she said they were. If I'm honest, I felt sorry for her. Gordon spent the whole time chatting to—"

Jasmin hesitated. Marjorie watched as the memory prompted a reaction.

"Who? Who was Gordon talking to?" Edna asked.

Jasmin shook her head. "Lots of people. Do you think the police would have told them?"

"I'm certain of it," said Marjorie. "The next of kin are always told first."

"What an awful job." Jasmin's face fell.

"The inspector interviewed people throughout yesterday, you said." Marjorie didn't want to focus on the morose, so she needed to stop Edna harking back to whoever it was Gordon had been speaking to the whole time at the get together.

"Yes, Inspector Bloom. That's a lovely name, but what a job. Has she spoken to you?"

"All except Fred," said Edna. "She might come back for him later. She interviewed me and Horace over breakfast."

Jasmin looked confused.

"She's teasing," said Marjorie. "The inspector was called away and didn't have time to interview Frederick."

"I didn't realise she'd already been today. Someone else must have let her in while I was speaking to David in the library."

That explained why Jasmin had told Marjorie the inspector would be coming back today when she had already been. Marjorie had been worried Jasmin had seen DI Bloom and forgotten about it.

Satisfied Jasmin was still lucid, Marjorie said, "I got the impression the inspector is being quite thorough in her questioning."

"She asked all sorts of things about Gordon and Oscar's relationship. There wasn't much I could tell her, apart from why Gordon was at the party the other night."

"Which was?" Horace asked.

"A personal matter, he said."

"Oh, really? I thought he told me it was a business matter," Edna said.

"It may have been," said Jasmin. "Business and personal can meld into one sometimes, can't they? If only he hadn't come. It's upset Oscar and David was out of sorts all day yesterday. He worries too much."

"David or Oscar?" Frederick asked.

"I was referring to David. Oscar's more volatile and lets his feelings out in anger, but David tends to fret. He's so protective of me, sometimes it's… it almost feels disloyal to say this, but sometimes it can be too much. Still, better to have someone care than not." Jasmin smiled, draining the last of the hot liquid from her cup.

"Is it just you he's worried about, or is something else on his mind?" Marjorie asked.

"He wouldn't tell me if there was. I know he and Oscar clash at times, but that's mainly because David feels Oscar puts on me with all his entertaining. He was furious about the other night."

"Leaving you to entertain his business associates and friends, you mean?" Marjorie asked.

"Yes, but I wanted to stay up anyway to see you after all these years, and Terry can look after himself. He's been coming here for long enough. He and Jamie get on."

"What about Paris? Where does she fit in?" Edna quizzed.

Marjorie noticed a flicker of a frown cross Jasmin's face. "She doesn't fit in at all. I can't work out why Oscar lets her stay so often. She all but lives here."

Horace raised a quizzical eyebrow in Marjorie's direction. Marjorie frowned. Perhaps Georgina wasn't the only woman having an affair.

"Speaking of Oscar, he's on his way again," said Edna. "I think our time's up."

"Perhaps we'd better let you get some rest," said Marjorie.

"I do feel rather tired," said Jasmin.

"I'll let John and Vic know we've finished," said Horace. "Can we do anything to help?"

"Perhaps Marjorie can pour me a drink of my herbal remedy. Oscar likes me to have three glasses a day."

"Of course, my dear." Marjorie got up hastily and made to follow Jasmin into her annexe, whispering to Edna,

"You head Oscar off while I do this. I'll catch up with you afterwards."

Chapter 21

Frederick was waiting for Marjorie on Jasmin's patio. Horace, Edna and Oscar were nowhere in sight.

"They got rid of him, then?"

"It wasn't easy, but Edna did her flirty thing and asked him to give them a personal tour of the grounds. What's that?"

"A glass of Jasmin's herbal remedy. I thought it might give me a pick-me-up. The past two days' shenanigans are catching up with me." Marjorie closed the conservatory doors and took a seat at the table, which had been cleared. She put the glass to her mouth.

"Just a minute," said Frederick, snatching it from her hand.

Marjorie was taken aback. "I could get you one if you like," she offered, but Frederick shook his head. He sniffed the liquid.

"Hmm, not sure," he said.

"Don't tell me you suspect Jasmin's being poisoned?" Marjorie knew Frederick had been a pharmacist all his working life.

He gazed at her with his deep grey eyes. "It has crossed my mind. I'd rather you didn't drink it until we've had it tested. From what you've told me about your friend's funny turn and what we witnessed over lunch, it could be arsenic toxicity. And if she's taking this stuff three times a day, what better way to administer a poison?"

Marjorie had to admit it was a possibility, although she hated the thought of it.

"So, Oscar Winchester is a killer?"

"Let's not jump to conclusions. It's only a theory. Your friend could have any number of conditions that would account for her lapses – early dementia, some neurological or other brain disease – but as she is the matriarch and most likely owns this place, her son could be losing patience with her longevity."

"We don't know the terms of her husband's will and it's not something I would feel comfortable asking her or Oscar about." Marjorie looked at the dark brown liquid in the glass.

"We could ask David Cribb," suggested Frederick.

"Not yet. If Jasmin is being poisoned, he might also be a suspect."

"I doubt it. He adores her and is devoted, from what I've seen."

"Agreed, but he might be a wonderful actor. We should ask DI Bloom to dig into that aspect of things and request she get this tested." Marjorie had just reached out to get a closer look at the glass when Oscar's voice drifted over to them, causing her to panic. The glass slipped from her hand and shattered on the paving slabs. Casper leapt from his bed and jumped over the wall.

"Blast!"

Marjorie could feel her heart lurch as she watched Oscar being dragged past them and back towards the house by Edna, with Horace following behind. Relief turned to annoyance. She could have kicked herself.

"That certainly woke the sleepy cat. Should I nip in and get some more?" Frederick asked as they watched the liquid evaporating under the scorching sun.

"I wouldn't want to wake Jasmin. Would a shard of glass be enough?" Marjorie asked.

"It might be. It's worth a try, but depends how diluted the solution is. I'd rather get a proper sample."

At that moment, John appeared. "Mr Winchester is asking for you both." Seeing the broken glass, he raised an eyebrow.

"It was me – a silly accident," said Marjorie. "We were going to clear it up."

"No need for that." He called back to Vic, who never seemed to be far away. "Bring a dustpan and brush, mate, would you?"

Marjorie sighed, and she and Frederick left the patio to head back to the house.

"Now what?" he asked.

"Either we call DI Bloom, tell her our suspicions and see if she'll send someone over, or I'll go back in a couple of hours and collect another sample to give to her. I'll ask Johnson to grab a small container from the kitchen."

"My vote is to tell the police," said Frederick.

"I'm inclined to agree with you," said Marjorie. "As long as DI Bloom takes us seriously."

"I'll tell her there was a strange smell."

"Was there?"

"Yes, but I couldn't detect arsenic; whatever's in that herbal drink is pungent. Now I think of it, I might be wrong about this. Maybe we'd better get a sample. I don't want to be accused of wasting police time."

Marjorie didn't want Patricia Bloom to be annoyed with them for wasting her precious time and resources either, when there might be nothing to Frederick's suspicion. "Okay, I'll text Johnson before we do anything. He might also have some information for us."

Marjorie tapped a message on her phone and waited.

"No reply. He might be with the kitchen staff. He'll get back to me when he picks this up."

"In which case, do you mind if we take a stroll in the gardens before going back inside?"

Marjorie hesitated before answering. "I don't think we can. Not now that John has delivered Oscar's message. I don't want the poor man to get into trouble, like his friend did yesterday when I didn't obey Oscar's summons. Perhaps afterwards."

Frederick's shoulders slumped, and the light went out of his eyes. "I suppose you're right. Hang on a minute... there's Oscar now, stomping outside in the opposite direction. There's no sign of Horace or Edna."

As she watched Oscar storming around to the other side of the house, Marjorie let out a heavy sigh. "It must be exhausting having a temper like his. He seems to be on the warpath again and has forgotten about us, so we'll do as you suggest. There's shade behind the trees over there where I thought I heard a fountain when I was looking for you yesterday. Edna mentioned seeing one from her window."

Seemingly in a hurry to get going before Marjorie changed her mind, Frederick took off at a pace towards the large elm trees. "Some stroll," she muttered, trying to keep up with her retreating friend.

Once they were hidden from view of any windows of the house, Frederick slowed down. Marjorie stopped, catching her breath and removing her walking stick from her handbag. She unfurled it and placed it in her right hand.

Frederick wiped sweat from his forehead with an initialled handkerchief. Marjorie couldn't help noticing its fine lace and saw the initials J.M. embroidered in the corner.

"It was my wife's. I always carried two, one for me and one for her. Just in case. She had a habit of getting hot chocolate on her top lip." Frederick looked down at the ground. "Old habits and all that."

"What a thoughtful thing to do." Not wanting to be unkind, Marjorie paused for a moment before suggesting they try the walk at a more leisurely pace.

Frederick grinned. "Sorry. This place makes me nervous. I don't like the way Oscar treats his mother and the more I think about it, the more I'm convinced if anyone's poisoning her, it'll be him."

"Do you imagine he's trying to kill her or keep her from interfering?" Marjorie asked, as they wandered along a rustic path.

"Either of those would fit. He could just want to keep her out of the way, but whether permanently or temporarily, who knows? It makes you wonder whether he didn't inherit."

Marjorie inhaled a deep breath. If this theory was true, Ralph had done a similar thing with his will, leaving Marjorie a controlling interest in the business to ensure their son, Jeremy, didn't fritter away everything on his next grand scheme or his extravagant wife.

"If that's the case," she said, "Hugh didn't trust Oscar. And if you're right about Oscar poisoning Jasmin, he had good reason not to." At least Marjorie herself had no worries on that score. Jeremy may not like her occasionally putting the brakes on his plans, but he went out of his way to ensure her safety at all times. He loved her, of that she had no doubt, and she loved him despite his weaknesses.

"Having met the man, I don't blame Hugh Winchester, but he may have put his widow in mortal danger. Better to lose money than one's life, if you ask me. He could have made sure she was well looked after without riling a ruthless son."

"We're hypothesising, though, aren't we? We don't know for sure that Jasmin is being poisoned or who got what in Hugh's will. For all we know, Jasmin could have an illness no-one but she and Oscar – and more than likely David – know about, and Oscar's being a doting son."

Frederick pulled a face. "You don't believe that for one minute," he said.

"I'd like to. Look! There's the fountain."

Frederick and Marjorie enjoyed some time wandering around the fountain and the grounds surrounding it. There was a calming sound of trickling water coming from the fountain and she heard a mower somewhere in the distance. Birds chirping their songs in the background rang through the air. The fountain was a work of art, its tiers of glittering water lit up as they cascaded into a magnificent pool. The grounds around were a lush green, dotted with tall beech trees, and rhododendrons and rose bushes seemed to whisper in the breeze. The sun was sparkling off the shiny rhododendron leaves, casting a beautiful light onto the compacted gravel path. Marjorie dipped her fingers in the fountain, feeling the coolness of the water on her fingertips and the smoothness of the stones.

"We'd better get back before anyone misses us," said Frederick. "Edna will give us an earful for wandering off without her."

Marjorie laughed. It had been a pleasant interlude.

"Time to face Oscar and find out if Johnson has discovered anything useful."

"Let's take the long way round," suggested Frederick.

Chapter 22

Johnson strolled around the Winchesters' sprawling estate. It was a humid summer day, but still perfect for displaying the grounds in all their glory, and the imposing grand manor house. After sitting in a rose garden for a while, he headed back towards the house, inhaling the aromatic air. He had agreed to assist Marjorie with her mission and was determined to help in any way he could.

The house was silent as he made his way down the stairs to the kitchen. He found Vic and John bringing in lunch trays.

"Would you like something to eat?" Vic had an easy going smile on his face and a lightness in his eye as he spoke. He gestured with his hands, as if offering Johnson a plate. His voice was warm and inviting, as if he and Johnson had known each other for years. There was nothing threatening about these two men, as far as he could tell.

"That would be great, thank you," Johnson replied. "Where's the chef?"

"He's nipped home to let his dog out," said John, the taller of the two men and the more serious. His voice was low and gravelly, adding even more seriousness to his already intense presence. He spoke in short sentences, his words ringing out with authority while Vic's flowed more easily and with more warmth.

"But we don't need him just now. There's plenty left over from your boss and her friends' lunch." Vic gestured at the untouched food on the trays.

"Mrs Winchester didn't eat much," said John.

"And we both know why," Vic growled.

The trio sat down and ate the leftovers from Mrs Winchester and Lady Marjorie's lunch. Johnson took the opportunity to pick up on what Vic had said.

"What did you mean about Mrs Winchester not eating?" he asked.

Vic and John exchanged glances before Vic spoke.

"Oscar came home early and interrupted them. The poor woman never gets a chance to enjoy herself."

Johnson filed that away in his brain asking, "What do you think of Oscar Winchester?"

"He's a decent enough boss, but—"

John finished Vic's sentence. "We don't like him very much."

Johnson nodded. They weren't telling him anything he hadn't observed, but it was useful to hear it from their mouths.

"We preferred it when his father was alive. Things were less tense and his mother was protected."

"Protected from what?" Johnson asked.

"Her son for one," said Vic.

"And the others," added John.

"What do you mean?" asked Johnson.

Vic shrugged. "Nothing. We don't mean nothing. It's just that now she can barely move without one of them putting a stop to it. She used to go out, but not anymore."

"It could be grief, though," said John, shooting a warning look towards his friend.

"Maybe, maybe not." Vic was in full flow again. "I don't think they'd allow it."

John's eyes looked worried. "Ignore us," he said to Johnson. "We don't mean anything. It's just that Mrs Winchester was the life and soul of this house—"

"Until Oscar ground her down," Vic snarled.

"I don't think Lady Marjorie's chauffeur needs to hear about the family's dirty linen," said John firmly.

Johnson changed the subject before either of them realised he was prying. "Dreadful thing, Lady Marjorie finding that body. She was quite upset by it."

"I'm not surprised. It's hardly your everyday occurrence, is it?" said John.

"Even in this strange house," added Vic.

"Did either of you notice anything unusual that night after I went to bed?"

Vic and John looked thoughtful for a moment. Then Vic spoke.

"I heard Gordon Collins having a heated conversation on the phone. It was pretty loud."

Johnson considered this. It was possible this conversation had something to do with Gordon's death.

"With Oscar, do you think?"

"Nah, sounded like a husband and wife type of barney to me. John would know all about them."

The tall man grimaced. "Yeah. Glad that's over. Getting a divorce was the best thing that ever happened to me. You married?"

Johnson felt the familiar pang. "Divorced."

"You know what I mean, then," said John.

"Not really. My wife and I never argued, but she suffered from depression all the years we were married. Then one day I got home from work and found a note."

"She left you?" Vic asked.

"Yeah. No explanation – just said I'd be better off without her. She went to live with her sister in Australia."

John looked sympathetic. "Did you try to get her back?"

Johnson shook his head. "I took to the bottle. I was in a bad way when Lord Snellthorpe – Lady Marjorie's late husband – found me drunk on a park bench."

"What? Just took you home, like?" Vic looked aghast.

"Sort of. Before the wife left, I was a plumber and had done a few jobs for him. He recognised me, sat down next to me, listened to my story. By then, the house was being repossessed because I hadn't been working. He told me there and then, if I sobered up, he'd got a vacancy for a chauffeur and a house I could rent."

Tears threatened when Johnson remembered the man who had become a close friend. "That's the kind of man he was, and his wife is just as good. I promised him if anything ever happened to him, I'd take good care of Lady Marjorie."

"He sounds amazing. You wouldn't find Oscar doing anything like that." Vic scowled.

"His dad might have done. Hugh Winchester was a good man. Gordon's dad and he were close," John said.

Johnson inwardly shook himself out of his reverie, remembering what he was doing here. "Did either of you see Gordon come down here on the night he died?"

"No. The boss was still out when we went up. Mrs Winchester was entertaining, and David told us we could go off duty. We played cards in Vic's room for a bit, then got some sleep."

Vic sighed. "We're worried about Mrs Winchester's health."

Johnson didn't get time to ask what in particular was worrying them because Kris, the chef, returned from letting his dog out.

"I've just bumped into Oscar. He wants you to tell Lady Marjorie and Mr Mackworth he wants to see them in the house."

John pushed himself up, using the table as a prop. "See you later."

Johnson thanked Vic and John for the lunch, and they left the kitchen. He observed Kris donning his white apron. The chef was tall and broad-shouldered with a mop of short, curly black hair and was cleanly shaven. His hands looked red and rough from years of kneading dough and handling hot pans.

"Am I in your way?"

"Not at all. No tennis today?"

"No. They stayed in today. I think Lady Marjorie wanted to catch up with her friend Mrs Winchester and check she was okay after the events of yesterday."

"It was chaotic yesterday. The police were here for hours and Oscar was doing his nut about anything and everything. I got most of the day off, as I wasn't allowed in the kitchen until dinnertime."

"Do you have any idea what happened the night before last?" Johnson felt he had the opening he needed.

"None. I went home after cooking dinner," Kris said. "As far as I know, Alison helped the guys clear up, and then she left. Vic and John are the only ones that sleep in. Them and Jamie, but you won't get anything out of Jamie. He thinks because he works for Oscar, he can throw his weight around. But if anyone knows anything, it'll be him. He sees everything and hears everything, if you know what I mean."

Johnson wondered if Kris meant Jamie would know what had happened or whether he was implying the bodyguard might be involved in some way. It was hard to tell.

"I suppose working so closely with Oscar Winchester puts him in a position to know most of what happens in the family, but according to Lady Marjorie, they were out until the early hours," said Johnson. "Did you know the dead man?"

"Nope, and what he was doing down here is a mystery. None of them have any reason to be downstairs. The police reckon he was murdered now, though, don't they?"

"Lady Marjorie mentioned that on the way to the tennis yesterday. She was quite traumatised. It's terrible."

"Makes me glad I don't live in now," said Kris.

"But who would do such a thing?" Johnson asked.

"Search me. Although word is that he was seeing the boss's Mrs."

"Seeing as in having an affair?" Johnson asked.

"Yeah, but it's only hearsay, some's saying he found out about it on the day you lot arrived. But don't go spreading it around, it might just be gossip. If it's true, though, it puts Oscar right up there as chief suspect number one. Can't say I'd mind if he was behind bars. The place would be a lot better run by Mrs Winchester and David."

Whilst Johnson was pleased to be uncovering the machinations behind the family's workings, the staff's lack of loyalty shocked him. Perhaps he was lucky to have worked for Lord Snellthorpe and then Lady Marjorie, who were wonderful people and employers. He felt slightly uncomfortable when he thought of Marjorie's son, Jeremy. Perhaps if he worked for him, he might feel like Vic, John and Kris.

He shook the thought from his mind. "As you say, it could just be idle gossip," he said, determined to tell Lady Marjorie what he had uncovered. He felt his phone vibrate in his pocket, but didn't want to distract himself from the conversation.

Alison, the house manager, joined them and the discussion with Kris ended. He set to work in the kitchen, while Alison gave Johnson a nod.

"Hello. You've had lunch, I see." The house manager stood tall with a slim figure and piercing green eyes. She had shoulder-length brown hair that fell in waves, and she moved around the kitchen with a confidence and poise which suggested she knew the house inside out.

As Alison sat down and poured herself a cup of tea, Johnson noticed how smooth her hands were and the neatly manicured nails. Her appearance hinted at an attention to detail that was hard to ignore.

Johnson answered her opening statement, smiling at her. "Yeah, Vic and John fed me. I'm at a bit of a loose end with my employer not going to tennis today," he said.

"That was an awful business, her finding Gordon like she did. How is she?"

"Bearing up. She's more worried about Mrs Winchester than herself."

"I take it you mean Mrs Winchester senior?"

"Yes," said Johnson.

"And well she might be. Such a nice man, Gordon was. He often came down here after having meetings with Oscar or David."

Johnson's ears pricked up. That was the opposite of what Kris, who was banging about looking for something in the pantry, had just told him.

"You knew him well, then?" Johnson asked.

"I wouldn't say well, but he wasn't above himself like some of Oscar's colleagues."

"Such as?"

"Terry Kemble for one. He used to be just a hanger-on, a friend from Oxford, but he's got all high and mighty since Oscar put him in charge of the Europeans."

Johnson knew about the European arm of the hotel chain and assumed that was what Alison was referring to. "I suppose some people get like that when they're promoted."

"Right stuck up, he is now. Mr Winchester senior would never have allowed it, I can tell you that for nothing." Kris continued to clatter around in the pantry, huffing and puffing about whatever it was he was looking for, and Alison added, "Gordon didn't like Terry either."

"What makes you say that?"

Alison jutted her chin out. "I saw him in Terry's room that night. He asked me not to mention it, said what he was looking for was important."

"Did he say what it was he was looking for?"

"No, I made myself scarce. I didn't want anyone knowing I knew he was rooting around in someone's bedroom. It doesn't really matter now, though, does it?"

"When was this?"

"After dinner. Terry and David were having a confab in Oscar's sitting room. I took them tea."

Kris came back at that moment, and Alison waved a hand across her throat. The conversation was over. Johnson could not ask whether Alison had told the police about finding Gordon in Terry Kemble's room. He felt it was time to leave them to it.

He checked his mobile for missed calls and saw a text from Lady Marjorie, asking him to get a sealable container from the kitchen.

"Time for me to go. Do you mind if I take a few strawberries with me?" he asked.

"Course not." Alison took a small plastic container from a cupboard and put some in for him. Hopefully, that would do. There was a lot to tell Lady Marjorie.

Johnson was about to go in search of his boss when he heard raised voices coming from outside. He poked his head through the open doors, but couldn't see anything, so he tiptoed down the steps and walked along the hedged driveway to the right, where the noise was coming from.

Before he could see who was arguing, he felt a sharp pain in the back of his head and everything went black.

Chapter 23

DI Bloom pushed through the half-open doors, barrelling past Horace and Edna, who were about to head outside to look for Marge and Fred. Vic was hovering in the hallway, tapping his foot.

Bloom turned on him and pointed a finger.

"Where is Oscar Winchester?"

"He went outside a while ago," Vic replied with a shrug. "I haven't seen him come back in."

"What about his wife? Where is she?" Bloom barked.

Vic held his palms outwards. "I don't know."

"Georgina went out," Horace said. "I believe Oscar left us to look for her."

"I see," said Bloom before turning back to Vic. "Perhaps you could call Oscar and ask him to come in. I need to speak to him *and* his wife."

Vic took out his mobile and lumbered outside to make the call.

"What is it?" Horace asked.

DI Bloom moved closer to him and Edna. "The dead man was having an affair with Oscar Winchester's wife, but nobody thought to tell us," she said, scrutinising them. "Just as I thought… you don't seem surprised."

"We only found out about the affair from Marge. She and Fred found the wife in bits in the garden after you told everyone about the murder yesterday morning," said Edna. "Georgina swore to Marge that her husband did not know about the affair. Marge was going to talk to her about telling you."

"Well, Marjorie and Georgina are wrong. These people have been wasting my time. Oscar Winchester knew about the affair. He had motive, opportunity and means. It's his house, after all. And what's more, he has no alibi for the early hours when the murder took place."

"But I heard him come home in the early hours of yesterday morning, and I'm sure he passed my room soon afterwards when he went to bed."

"That may be, but unless you were in the room with him all night, Mr Tyler, it doesn't mean a thing. Not to mention it could have been anybody passing your room that night. He and his wife have been sleeping in separate rooms. We already know that."

"Yes, but—"

"There's no but about it. I can recognise when someone is hiding something and I know when people are lying to me. The man's taking us for fools. He's been misdirecting us at every turn, trying to send us into a maze with his lies while pointing the finger at everyone except himself. I've got enough evidence to hold him for questioning, and that's what I intend to do."

"You said no-one told you about the affair. How did you find out?" Horace asked.

"Not from my inside sources, that's for sure," she snapped, glaring at them.

"That's hardly fair," said Edna. "Marge would have told you this morning, but you were called away to a post mortem, remember?"

DI Bloom smiled for the first time since barging in. She took a deep breath.

"You're right. I'm sure you would have told the police… eventually. Instead, we found out from another reliable source. It appears Mrs Collins has suspected her husband of playing away for some time, and had hired a private investigator. Now between you and me, Mrs Collins told us she informed Oscar Winchester on the morning you arrived, before the murder took place."

Edna felt her jaw drop open. "So he did know about it all along? No wonder he seemed angry when we arrived that day and was nasty to his wife. That's why he changed their arrangements. It might also explain what he and Jamie were arguing about that night."

"When?" DI Bloom stared with disbelief.

Horace flushed red, clearing his throat. "I saw the two of them arguing after they arrived home in the early hours of yesterday. It didn't seem relevant."

"When will you people learn I decide what's relevant?" said the inspector, looking angrier by the minute. "I'm relying on you not to mention a word of this conversation to anyone in this house."

"You can rest assured on that point," said Horace.

"How come you only found out about all this today?" Edna quizzed.

"It appears Mrs Collins didn't want to sully her husband's name when she heard someone had killed him, but after a sleepless night, she wondered if it had been her telling Oscar Winchester that had been the catalyst. Now she can't forgive herself."

"It's hardly her fault if Oscar decides to snuff out the competition, is it?"

DI Bloom shrugged. "You have a way with words, Edna. Where is your leader and chief, by the way?"

"If you mean Marjorie, we were just on our way to look for her. Oscar summoned her and Fred before he went off in a huff after having a word with Jamie. He said he had urgent business to attend to. That's when we overheard Jamie telling him his wife had left the house with his car keys. He ran out of here like a demented rabbit. She'd been out shopping all morning as well."

"Yeah, so, we assumed she'd had enough and was going to leave him, but she told Marge yesterday morning that wasn't an option. Unless, of course, she's found out Oscar knew about the affair and thinks he killed Gordon."

"In which case, we had better find her before he does," said DI Bloom.

"You might be too late, but we'll help," said Horace.

"The only way you can help now is by staying out of the way. Blaby! Call for backup and search the grounds. We need to find Oscar Winchester."

"Be careful," said Edna. "He might have a gun."

DI Bloom pivoted on the spot. "What?"

"His bodyguard owns a gun. He could have it or he might have enlisted him. Jamie went out shortly after him."

Tensing, the inspector flicked the hair from her deep blue eyes, which were wide and alert, her mouth set in a grim line. At last she spoke.

"This day just can't get any worse." Her hand tightened around her radio as she took it out of her handbag. She pressed a button and called dispatch, her voice tight and shrill as she called for more backup. "Possible armed suspect at Hallenguard Manor. Please send AFOs, stat."

Static hissed from the radio, and then they heard help was on its way.

"What are AFOs?" asked Horace.

"Authorised firearms officers," Bloom replied.

"I'm not saying he definitely has a gun on him, so tell them not to go firing their weapons willy-nilly," said Edna.

If a look could have melted ice, DI Bloom shot one in Edna's direction.

"Just stay inside. If anybody else comes down, keep them here."

"But what about Marjorie?" Horace called after the retreating inspector, who didn't reply. He rubbed his forehead. "If she's got any sense, she'll stay hidden once she sees the armed response team."

"This is Marge we're talking about," muttered Edna. "You know she'll stick her nose in and put herself in danger. We need to find her."

DI Bloom was outside, yelling instructions into her radio. She had left DC Sudhik at the front door.

"We can get out through the kitchen. Johnson might be down there. We'll get him to help. You try phoning her." Horace's voice had a sense of urgency in it, which Edna rarely heard from him.

"Knowing her, she won't have her bloomin' phone on. I'll try Fred." Edna hurried after Horace, puffing with stress and from the exertion. While on the move, she dialled Fred's phone. "It's gone straight to voicemail. I'll try Marge."

Horace wasn't listening. He was on a mission. Edna stopped in the kitchen, noticing a startled looking man and woman staring after him.

"What's going on?" the woman asked.

"The police are here. They're looking for Oscar. The inspector has called in armed police just in case he's got Jamie's gun. You'll need to stay indoors. Have you seen Johnson, Marge's chauffeur?"

"You must be one of Lady Marjorie's friends," said the woman. "I'm Alison, manager of the house."

It's hardly the bloomin' time for introductions, thought Edna. "So, have you seen him?"

"He went to look for Lady Marjorie, I think, but he might equally have gone for a lie down."

"Thanks a lot," Edna huffed, getting through to Marge's voicemail. "Marge, if you get this message, stay where you are and text me or Horace with your whereabouts."

By the time Edna got outside, Horace was turning the corner on the west side of the house. Edna moved as fast as she could, but these days that wasn't so quick. Her chest felt like it would explode at any minute and the extra weight she was carrying was playing havoc with her knees.

Still, she persevered, determined to find Marge before she put herself in danger.

When she turned the corner, her eyes bulged.

"What the—"

Chapter 24

As Frederick and Marjorie neared the east side of the house, she heard a sound like a moan coming from behind a laurel hedge.

"Did you hear that?"

Frederick stopped, listening. The groaning sound came again.

"Wait there," he said.

Marjorie had no intention of waiting anywhere and followed Frederick through a gap in the hedge.

"Johnson! What on earth happened?"

Johnson was sitting on the ground, rubbing the side of his head where there was a lump the size of a golf ball. He squinted up at them.

"I heard shouting, then someone hit me from behind," he muttered.

Frederick went to help him to his feet. "Can you stand?"

"Yes, I think so. I'll be all right in a few minutes. I think I must have been unconscious." Johnson swayed, steadying himself by holding onto Frederick's arm.

"In which case, we need to call for an ambulance and get you to the hospital," said Marjorie.

Johnson grimaced. "I'm sure that won't be necessary."

Ignoring his protestations, Marjorie reached in her handbag for her phone. "I have a missed call from Edna. I expect Oscar's back inside and growing impatient."

"There's an awful lot of activity over there," said Frederick, who had moved back to the gap in the hedge. Marjorie moved behind him and watched numerous police cars and a van parking up.

"Good heavens. Are those police officers armed?"

Johnson, seeming more alert now, joined them. "Something serious is going on. You'd better check that message from Edna."

The police appeared to be sweeping the other side of the grounds. Armed officers were taking positions from various vantage points. Marjorie dialled her voicemail and listened.

"She says to stay where we are and let her and Horace know where that is." Marjorie replayed the message for Frederick and Johnson to hear.

221

"She sounds stressed. I bet that Jamie fellow's gone over the edge and is on the rampage with his gun," said Frederick. "Why they give people like him licences, I'll never understand."

Marjorie didn't feel it was fair to judge a man they had hardly met, but Frederick might have a point. Jamie appeared to be a loose cannon waiting to go off.

"I'll message Edna and tell her where we are," she said.

Before she got the chance to do so, there was a commotion and they watched an ambulance with flashing blue lights racing up the driveway. DI Bloom emerged from the far side of the house with Oscar, who was in handcuffs. A police officer was frantically waving at the paramedics to follow him back that way.

Marjorie, Frederick and Johnson watched as Oscar was shoved into a waiting police car and the armed officers returned to their van. DI Bloom barked orders to uniformed officers before getting into a car herself. A police cordon was erected between two trees.

"That doesn't look good," said Frederick.

"No, it doesn't," Marjorie agreed.

"We should tell the police about your attack, Johnson."

Johnson shook his head. "I don't think now's a good time. We don't know what's going on."

Marjorie felt he was right. "The police look a bit tied up at the moment. Let's speak to them later. In the meantime, Johnson, you need to get to the hospital."

"Fine, but I'm not going in an ambulance. I'll drive," Johnson answered.

"Why don't I take you?" offered Frederick.

Marjorie was grateful they had avoided an argument. Johnson could be stubborn when it came to healthcare. She couldn't remember the last time he'd visited a doctor.

"Would you like me to come too?" she asked.

"No. You stay here and find out what's happened. Edna and Horace will be worrying about where we are," said Frederick.

The trio strolled back towards the house now that the police had moved their vehicles over to where the cordon was being set up. Johnson handed the car keys to Frederick.

"Oh, this is for you," he said, reaching into his pocket. He handed Marjorie a small container of strawberries.

Marjorie was confused. "Thank you, Johnson, but I'm not very hungry."

He grinned. "Sorry. You asked for a container and it was the best I could get. I was with Kris and Alison in the kitchen, so I asked for some strawberries, hoping Alison would give me a container. I couldn't think of a good enough excuse to get an empty one."

"Oh. Good thinking, Johnson. Thank you." Marjorie placed the container with its contents in her handbag.

She watched as Frederick drove away until the car was out of sight. She could ask Johnson what he remembered about his attack later, and whether he had found out anything from Oscar's employees. The priority was to rule out concussion.

Looking at the phone in her hand, Marjorie couldn't remember what she had been about to do before they had witnessed Oscar being taken away by the police. She put it back in her handbag and walked up the steps into the house.

David Cribb was in the hall, dishing out orders to Vic and John when she entered. "Find Jamie. I need to speak to him urgently. He's got to be around somewhere. He's never far away from Oscar."

The two men headed outside, nodding to Marjorie as they passed. David had turned-heel and gone downstairs to the kitchen. Marjorie saw the door to Oscar's sitting room was ajar. She heard voices and walked in. Terry and Paris stopped speaking when she went inside.

"Did I just see the police taking Oscar away?" she asked, playing the innocent.

"There's been another murder. At least, that's what it looks like," said Terry.

"Good grief! Who?"

"The police haven't said, but we think it was Georgina," said Paris. "She's been having an affair with Gordon and Oscar found out."

"I see," Marjorie said. "And you think Oscar killed her because of it?"

Paris shook her head and frowned. Her eyes narrowed as she considered the situation.

"Oscar wouldn't kill anyone," she said.

"So why have the police arrested him, then?" Terry challenged with a sarcastic tone before he stood up and stormed out of the room, slamming the door behind him.

After Terry left, Marjorie looked at Paris, her mind full of questions. "Why don't you believe Oscar is a murderer?" she asked.

Paris shifted uncomfortably in her seat, and Marjorie could tell that she was hiding something. She had a feeling that it was more than just an opinion on the matter; it was personal.

"I know Oscar," Paris began slowly. "He's a passionate, sometimes volatile man, but that doesn't mean he's capable of murder. He's also a man of honour and would never do anything to hurt someone he cared about." She paused for a moment, looking away from Marjorie before continuing. "Oscar wouldn't be surprised if Georgina was having an affair – a dent in his pride, that's all. I can assure you, the police have got this wrong. Oscar is innocent."

Marjorie was still suspicious about Paris's relationship with Oscar, but decided not to push the issue any further. She knew there was more to her story than she was saying, but wasn't sure if it had anything to do with Oscar's innocence or Paris's belief in it. Marjorie decided to keep an eye on Paris as the investigation progressed and see if she could uncover whether there was any rationale behind why Paris didn't believe Oscar was guilty.

"Why was Terry so angry just now?" she asked.

"I expect he's got his own secrets, and he seems terrified the police will uncover whatever it is he's trying to hide," Paris said ominously.

"What kind of secrets?" Marjorie asked.

Paris shifted in her seat once more, her eyes suspicious. "I don't know any specifics, but I think Gordon knew something. I was told that after dinner the night before last, Gordon disappeared for ages. When he came downstairs again, he went straight for Terry and they argued."

Marjorie held Paris's gaze. "Who is your source?"

Paris clamped her lips shut, her brow furrowed. "I can't say."

"That all sounds very mysterious," said Marjorie. "You must have your own suspicions."

Paris eyed Marjorie. "Put it this way, I heard talk there was concern about the amount of money disappearing from the European hotel chain. I'm not sure if Gordon and Oscar argued about it."

"So you and your source believe Gordon was looking for evidence on the night of his death. But that still doesn't explain why he arrived in the first place asking to speak to Oscar, does it?"

"Perhaps not, but Terry's worried about something. He's like a coiled spring."

Before either of them got the chance to say anything else, Marjorie heard Edna's voice heading their way. The door burst open.

"You're never going to believe it, Marge."

Chapter 25

The first thing Edna saw was Oscar kneeling on the ground, gripping a bloodied knife in his right hand. He cradled Georgina's lifeless body in his arms, his soft sobs the only sound.

Horace stood a few feet away, cautiously moving closer. He put a finger to his lips, signalling Edna to be quiet. She held her breath.

"Best if you put the knife down, Oscar," Horace said gently, his words hanging in the air. But Oscar didn't move, apart from his body trembling as he let out muffled sobs.

Horace took another tentative step closer, bending down. Before turning to Edna with a grim expression, he placed his fingers on the young woman's neck.

"There's a pulse. Quick! Call an ambulance."

The next second, armed police surrounded them. Two of them pointed their guns at Oscar.

"Put the weapon on the floor. Now!" one shouted.

Edna grabbed the arm of an unarmed police officer. "Get an ambulance. She's alive!" The officer turned his back on her and muttered urgently into his radio.

Meanwhile, Oscar had looked up, his face a mask of confusion and shock. His hands were shaking as he laid Georgina down and let go of the weapon. It clattered to the ground. Edna recognised it as one of the ornamental daggers that had been hanging in the hall.

The police officers moved in quickly and handcuffed Oscar, dragging him to his feet. He seemed dazed and confused, mumbling, "I didn't do this… I found her." He repeated the words over and over again as they pulled him away from Georgina, but the police weren't listening. An armed officer gripped his cuffed wrists behind his back.

DI Bloom arrived at the scene. Her eyes blazed when she spotted Edna and Horace.

"I thought I told you two to stay inside," she said, shaking her head.

Two officers shoved Horace out of the way and began administering first aid to the woman lying on the ground. Edna was relieved to hear an ambulance siren coming closer. DI Bloom looked at Georgina and the officers, one of whom was holding something over the wound.

"How is she?"

"Not good. We need the paramedics."

"Keep doing what you're doing. They'll be here any minute." Bloom took hold of Oscar, turning to Edna and Horace. "I'll need to speak to you two again later." Then she led Oscar, who still looked bewildered, away.

Edna had never seen anyone so young looking so pale before, and she had frozen. Her mind was racing, trying to make sense of what she was witnessing. Frenetic activity was now taking place around the woman lying on the ground. All Edna could focus on was how ghostly Georgina Winchester looked, as if her life was ebbing away.

Two paramedics arrived carrying a stretcher and attended her. The two police officers who had administered the initial first aid looked hopelessly at each other, their hands coloured red.

Horace took Edna's arm. "I think we'd better go," he whispered.

Edna trembled. "I don't think I can walk," she said.

"Don't faint on me, Edna. It's the shock. We can take it steady."

Horace supported her as they started to make their way from the scene. They had barely gone two paces when Edna felt herself sliding towards the ground. A pair of muscular arms caught her, gathering her up as though she were a feather. She looked into the gnarled face and recognised it.

"Jamie, where did you come from?"

Ignoring her, Jamie spoke to Horace. "Follow me."

He carried Edna away from the tumultuous scene, walking along a path at the side of the house and moving around the back. Jamie stopped outside a stable door, gesturing for Horace to open it. They went into a small room with basic furniture and an unlit wood burner. He laid Edna down on a sofa.

"I'll get you a glass of water," he said.

"Thank you," Horace replied. "Where are we?"

"This is the old servants' snug. Alison and the others hide in here sometimes when they need to get away for a bit."

Edna downed the glass of water and felt much better. "Thanks for helping out just now; I thought I was a goner."

Jamie smiled weakly, asking, "What happened out there?"

"The police believe Oscar stabbed Georgina," Horace said.

"He would never do that," Jamie said firmly. He paced the small room, deep in thought, running a hand through his short fair hair.

Horace sighed. "We found him kneeling over her with a knife in his hand. I think the evidence is pretty damning," he said.

Jamie shook his head. "No. He wouldn't… he had no reason to."

"What about the affair between her and Gordon?" Edna challenged.

"And what about all Oscar's affairs?" Jamie burst out laughing. "They both knew the score. Stay together for the sake of upper-class appearances and do what they like as long as they are discreet. Georgina had kept her vows until this, but Oscar wouldn't kill her over it." He continued pacing back and forth.

"But Georgina told Marge she was in love with the bloke," said Edna.

"Gordon was married. He would never leave his kids, and Georgina might have thought she was in love with the guy, but she loves money more."

"As you say, Georgina had not strayed before. Maybe your boss believes it's all right for men to play away, but not women," Edna said. "We were told Oscar didn't find out until the day we arrived and he was pretty awkward with his wife on that day."

"Yeah, he was furious about it. Oscar viewed Gordon as a mere employee, which, in a way, he was. It would be like finding out I was having an affair with her – irritating, but not the end of the world. And not enough reason to stab her. I think he was more disappointed because he trusted Gordon."

"So what about killing Gordon, then? Was he angry enough to do that?" Horace asked.

Jamie frowned. "He said stuff, but he wouldn't go through with it. Oscar's all mouth. If he wanted to kill anyone, he'd get someone else to do it."

"Someone like you," said Edna.

"Yeah, maybe." Jamie grinned. "But he'd have to pay me a lot more than he does right now. Look, if you're feeling better, I'd better go. I've got some things to do before word spreads."

Edna and Horace watched as Jamie left. "Blimey, that guy's strong. I bet you couldn't have carried me like that," Edna teased.

Horace laughed. "I might have managed a couple of seconds." Then he looked thoughtful.

"What did you think of Oscar's reaction back there? Did you believe him?" Edna asked.

Horace shook his head. "He seemed convincing, but it's hard to imagine anyone else wanting to stab Georgina. By all accounts, her only sin was an affair."

"Which was acceptable if Jamie's to be believed," Edna said. "Though not with the accountant. I'll never get families like this."

Horace walked over to the window, looking outside. "No-one else other than Gordon's widow would have a motive to attack Georgina. Oscar did look shaken, though."

"You would be if you'd just stabbed somebody, wouldn't you?" Edna said.

Horace took Edna's glass and refilled it from the water dispenser Jamie had used. He poured himself one while he was at it.

"True. I'm still shaken, and I had nothing to do with it."

Edna shuddered. "I'd rather not think about what we saw." She took the water from Horace and knocked it back. "I wish it was a Scotch."

Horace clinked glasses with her. "We can pretend."

Edna smiled, but her heart was still racing. "Do you think she'll live?"

"It's hard to say. She looked to be in a bad way, the pulse was thready."

"Bloom got away smartish, didn't she?"

"I guess she was more concerned with making the arrest and getting the perpetrator away from the scene. Her officers seemed to know what they were doing."

"At least Marge didn't get caught up in any of it. Where do you think she's got to?"

Horace gave a sly grin.

"Don't be daft, Horace Tyler. I tease her about her and Fred, but they are just friends. Besides, she's too old to go off on a romantic escape, especially here."

"Maybe they stayed with Jasmin. They were still there when you manhandled Oscar back to the house after our tour."

"That's another thing that's been bothering me," said Edna. "Why do you think Oscar was so snappy with his mother? All she was doing was having lunch with an old friend."

Horace thought for a moment. "It was rather odd behaviour. Maybe there's something Oscar's hiding from his mother, something she wouldn't approve of. Or he was being overprotective—"

"More like controlling," finished Edna. "And if it's the latter, why?"

"Hopefully, we'll find out this evening. With Oscar out of the way, there'll be a lot less tension in the air."

"I can't believe you've just said that. How can there be less tension? There's been one murder, possibly two. Jasmin's son's been arrested, Jamie might decide it's time to bring out his gun again, and David Cribb will be like a mother hen clucking over Jasmin."

Horace stroked his chin. "You're quite right. I'm not thinking straight. It's not every day one sees such things."

He rinsed their glasses in a corner sink, leaving them to drain. "How do you feel?"

"Better. Let's find Marge. If the killer has been arrested, she might decide it's time to leave." Edna hoped, rather than believed, that Marge would agree.

"What about consoling Jasmin?"

"I'm sure she can do that from a distance. I don't want to stay here any longer." Edna meant it. There was an air of menace in Hallenguard Manor that made her want to run to the hills.

Chapter 26

Edna's face was flushed from the exertion of bursting into Oscar's sitting room. She was panting, cheeks puffing out and her chest heaving with each rapid breath. The black wig she was wearing today was tangled. Her eyes were wide, but she didn't say anything following her initial outburst, having noticed Paris's presence.

Paris stood up. "I'm going to speak to that policewoman and put her straight." Without another word, she strode towards the door, the skirt of her dress fluttering as she marched out.

Horace, who had entered behind Edna, quickly closed the door after Paris left. He looked at Marjorie.

"I take it, from that exhibition, you've heard the news already?"

Marjorie was still concerned over Edna's laboured breathing, but switched to focus on Horace's question. "That Oscar's been arrested? Yes, Frederick and I saw him being put into a police car in handcuffs. Paris said someone else has been murdered – she thinks it might be Georgina."

Edna's face paled as she spoke, her voice quivering. "We saw her. She was stabbed," she muttered.

Marjorie felt her eyes widening. "My goodness!"

"We found Oscar kneeling over his wife with one of them ornamental knives in his hand, and then there were armed police everywhere and they took him away... Bloom called for them when we told her he might be armed and all that... Jamie helped us... Oscar reckoned he found her there... she looked like an angel... I nearly fainted..." Edna's words were tumbling out in between shallow breaths. Then the room fell silent, other than Edna gasping every so often.

Horace sighed heavily and shook his head, a sorrow in his eyes Marjorie hadn't seen before. He crossed the room, his movements slow and deliberate while he filled a glass with whisky from a decanter on the side table and handed it to Edna. He sat next to her, taking her hand.

"Breathe, Edna. Drink this." Turning to Marjorie, he said, "She's had a terrible shock. We both have."

The smell of whisky filled the air, its odour bringing with it a warmth and calm. Edna sipped at first, and then gulped half of it down in one go.

Marjorie broke the silence. "Why don't you start again from the beginning?"

Horace signalled to Edna to hush while he spoke. "We were about to come looking for you and Fred."

"Where is he?" Edna interrupted, ignoring Horace's instruction. "I can't face going over this story too many times. Bloom's already said she wants to interview us again. She saw us at the scene – she's not happy with any of us, I can tell you that much."

"Frederick's gone out with Johnson. I'll explain more about that when Horace has finished." Marjorie didn't feel it was the right time to bring up Johnson's attack or ask why DI Bloom wasn't happy with them, fearing it might confuse matters.

Horace continued, "We were about to come looking for you when DI Bloom turned up. She had found out about Gordon's affair with Georgina and was annoyed we hadn't told her about it."

"Ah." Marjorie felt a slight wave of guilt wash over her. "I suppose it was inevitable. I haven't seen Georgina since yesterday morning," she said.

"Anyway, she found out because Gordon's wife had grown suspicious and hired a private investigator to discover if he was having an affair."

Marjorie's mind raced as she tried to process the information. "Paris admitted to me that Oscar had found out. I assume it was from Mrs Collins?" she said.

"Yes. So DI Bloom explained she had enough reason to take him in for questioning – obviously she suspected he had murdered Gordon and was keen to make an arrest. Edna warned her that if Oscar was in a rage, he might have armed himself – and told her there was a gun in the house. That's when she called in the armoury."

Marjorie thought for a few minutes. "And then she found he had also killed Georgina."

"May have. Georgina's still alive."

"Yeah, Horace found a pulse and the ambulance crew came and took over from the police."

"This all happened while they were arresting Oscar."

"Will she live?" Marjorie asked.

Horace held his palms uppermost. "She was barely alive."

"And now they have arrested Oscar."

"Yeah, so case wrapped up. Can we leave now?" The whisky had perked Edna up and she looked hopefully in Marjorie's direction.

Horace patted her on the shoulder. "Jamie insists Oscar has had a few affairs himself and that it wouldn't have been taboo in their marriage."

"He also said Oscar was furious about her having an affair with his accountant," Edna snapped. "Too lowly, it would appear."

"Jamie mentioned Oscar wouldn't be so rash as to kill anyone himself; that if he wanted someone dead, he would get someone else to do the deed."

"Interesting," said Marjorie. "Paris said more or less the same thing – not the latter part – but I suspect she and Oscar may be having an affair."

Edna gawped. "Bloomin' 'eck, what's wrong with these people?"

Horace gave a half-smile. "It's hard to know who's telling the truth."

"You're both forgetting something. Whatever Jamie, Paris or the man in the moon thinks, we found Oscar holding the knife with her blood all over it. It was horrible, Marge." Edna held her empty glass out to Horace for a refill.

Having obliged Edna with a second whisky, Horace sat next to her and said softly, "But we didn't see him stab her." He looked at Marjorie. "He swore he found her like that."

"Well, he would, wouldn't he?" snapped Edna. "He's not the type to admit to it."

"It appears to be case closed," conceded Marjorie. A nagging guilt crept through her as she wondered whether, had she told DI Bloom about the affair, Georgina might not have been attacked. She shook the thought from her head. There would be plenty of time for recriminations and soul-searching later.

Instead, she continued, "We know now that Oscar had motive, means and opportunity for Gordon's murder and the attack on his wife. One thing I would like to know is where was Jamie while all this was going on? He's usually there in the background somewhere."

"Good point, Marge, and it was him we heard telling Oscar Georgina had run off with the car keys. That's when he went tearing after her. Someone must have told her Oscar knew about the affair. My guess is she concluded Oscar had killed her lover and was running for her life."

"It explains why Frederick and I saw Oscar rushing around the side of the house after sending John to summon us inside. We didn't see Georgina, or Jamie, for that matter, but we didn't hang around. We went for a walk. Frederick needed some fresh air."

"There is another thing," said Horace. "Oscar wasn't carrying a knife when he stormed off."

"Not that we saw. He could have grabbed it on his way out. They hang on the wall, don't they?" Edna looked forlorn. Marjorie wasn't sure how much more she could take.

"Was it a large knife?"

"Quite big. More of a dagger, I'd say – about this length." Horace held his forefingers about eight inches apart. "Did you see him carrying it?"

Marjorie shook her head. "I'm afraid not, but we only got the briefest of glimpses. He was stomping in the opposite direction to where we were standing."

"You were going to tell us where the good man Frederick went to," Horace said. "And did Johnson find out anything?"

Marjorie rubbed her forehead. Something wasn't right about the whole fiasco.

"I'm afraid I didn't get the opportunity to ask him. Frederick and I found Johnson behind a hedge just before the big van full of police turned up. He'd been hit over the head and knocked out. Frederick's taken him to the hospital to get checked out."

Edna's eyes popped. "Now you see why we should leave. This place is lethal."

"Not any longer, Edna, if Oscar is the killer. It stands to reason he could have hit Johnson over the head," Horace said.

"Johnson told us he heard shouting just before someone hit him."

"If that was Oscar and Georgina, it can't have been Oscar who hit him," said Horace.

"The timings are out, anyway. We saw Oscar a good half an hour before finding Johnson. Although I can't say how long Johnson had been unconscious. Maybe Jamie and Oscar are in cahoots, or it could be something unrelated."

Horace frowned. "But why would Jamie get involved in murder?"

"Good old-fashioned money, I expect," Marjorie said. "The question we should ask is why would Jamie do anything for a man he clearly hates, and why protect him now that he's been arrested?"

"He lifted me like I was made of foam," said Edna.

Marjorie was confused. "You've lost me, I'm afraid."

"After Oscar was arrested, Edna almost fainted. Thank God, Jamie arrived just in time to catch her," said Horace. "He carried her away from the scene and led us to an old servants' snug where staff go when they want to hide – according to Jamie."

Marjorie felt her eyes scrunch, trying to follow the threads.

"What I'm saying, Marge, is Jamie would be strong enough to string that fella Gordon up. Know what I mean?"

"Now I see what you're getting at," said Marjorie. "Although anyone could have lured Gordon down to the scullery, strangled him and tied a rope around his neck. These old Victorian hangers were made to carry sodden washing and the pulley system would have done the bulk of the lifting. Even a strong woman with enough determination could have done the deed."

Edna pouted. "Either way, I vote we let the police handle it from now. They've got Oscar, and if Jamie's involved, they'll soon piece it together. Besides, DI Bloom ain't gonna take much more interference from us."

Marjorie's hand flew to her mouth. "Jasmin! I bet no-one's told Jasmin. David was in the house dishing out orders when I came in after Frederick and Johnson left. He sent Vic and John in search of Jamie. I wonder if he also suspects the bodyguard's involvement."

"If he does, he could be in danger. I don't think Jamie will go down lightly," said Horace. "We'd better find David."

"Yeah, you do that. I'll stay here and drink whisky. Let me know when you're done," said Edna, looking tired.

"I have to speak to Jasmin," said Marjorie, closing her eyes in concentration, "and find out about the poison, and then there's Terry and his suspected embezzling."

"Now you've lost me," said Horace.

Marjorie opened her eyes. Horace and Edna were staring at her as if she was from another planet.

Chapter 27

Marjorie was delighted when the door opened and Frederick joined them. His gentle eyes made her feel secure. His voice was soothing.

"Paris Toliver told me I'd find you in here. I went to the place they call the entertainment lounge. There's a lot of shouting going on in there."

"Are David and Jamie in the entertainment lounge?" Marjorie asked.

"David is. Along with Paris, Terry, Vic and John, but no Jamie, and no Jasmin."

"At least David's safe for now," said Horace. Looking at Frederick, he explained, "Oscar's been arrested."

"We saw that before I drove Johnson to the hospital. The cordon the police were putting up is all erected now and there's a forensics van and still a lot of police activity outside. What happened?"

Marjorie summarised what had happened since he'd left but, noticing Edna paling again, she kept the details about Georgina to the bare minimum.

Frederick's grey eyes appeared glazed. "So awful; I hope she'll recover. She's so beautiful."

Edna bristled, shooting him an annoyed look. "What's that got to do with anything?"

"Nothing. I don't know why I said it." Frederick looked down at the floor.

Feeling more tension building and worried Edna was about to give Frederick what for, Marjorie asked, "How's Johnson?"

"Fine. He's got one hell of a lump on his bonce, as he called it, and he's not happy they insisted he stay in overnight for concussion checks, but other than that, it shouldn't be serious. They've moved him to a head injury bay where they kept coming back, shining lights in his eyes and suchlike, asking him if he had a headache." Frederick grinned. "He told them he would have if they kept shining torches in his eyes."

"Good. If he's complaining, it sounds as though he'll be fine," said Marjorie, relieved. "He doesn't like hospitals."

Frederick smiled again. "So he said… Oh, and the sister in A&E called the police. We had no choice but to tell them how the injury happened."

"I would expect no less," said Marjorie.

"Johnson was keen for me to come back and tell you what he'd uncovered. He managed to get it out of Vic and John that they don't like, or trust, Oscar, and they are worried about his mother – Vic more than John, but it concurs with our concerns for her safety."

Edna opened her mouth to speak, but Marjorie gave a gentle shake of the head.

Frederick continued his report. "Kris wasn't much help, except his story and Alison's differ slightly. Kris said Gordon would have no reason to be downstairs and never ventured that way, whereas Alison said he often popped down and that he was friendly. She doesn't like Terry Kemble, says he's got too high and mighty for her liking."

"There could be an innocent explanation for the stories differing. Perhaps Kris wasn't around when Gordon was downstairs."

"My thoughts exactly," Frederick agreed. "The only interesting thing… well, two things. The first was that Alison discovered Gordon rooting around in Terry's room after dinner on the night of the murder. He asked her not to mention it and told her he was looking for something important."

Marjorie perked up. "Now that is interesting. Paris suspects someone, most likely Terry, has been helping themselves to company finances, but she wasn't clear whether Gordon and Oscar argued about it, which would imply Oscar may have suspected Gordon was involved. To be honest, she wasn't making much sense. But she said Gordon went missing for a while after dinner that night, so those two stories check out."

"Gordon could have been the one doing the embezzling and he was trying to plant evidence in Terry's room. Terry could have found it and done Gordon in himself," Horace suggested.

"Or Terry knew Gordon was going to tell Oscar what he'd found and killed him before he could do it. Paris says she saw Gordon have a row with Terry when he joined the others in the main room." Marjorie scrunched her eyes.

Edna rubbed her head. "This is killing me. So now we have more potential killers for Gordon? It's worse than an opera."

"Do you think Terry could have suspected Gordon told Georgina what he was up to? The affair seems to be the worst kept secret, from what I can gather," said Frederick. "Word is – also from Johnson – that Oscar knew about the affair. He found out on the morning we arrived."

"Alas, we've established that fact. Mrs Collins had hired a private detective," said Marjorie.

Frederick looked disappointed.

"Jamie – and others, it appears – is convinced Oscar would have suffered wounded pride about the affair and nothing more." Marjorie paused. "I'm not quite ready to believe Jamie's side of the story yet. He could still be the sole or joint killer."

"What about Vic and John? We haven't included them," said Edna, voice dripping with sarcasm. "Or Jasmin, for that matter."

"Now you are delving into the realms of fantasy. She's far too ill." Marjorie felt irritated that Edna would say such a thing, even in jest.

Edna's eyes narrowed. "The weakling thing could be an act."

"It's unlikely," said Horace, "but we need to put everything out there, no matter how ridiculous."

Edna had been about to gloat, but glared at Horace. "How come my ideas are ridiculous and everyone else's theories are possible?" Her lips pouted. Marjorie changed the subject.

"Frederick believes someone is trying to poison Jasmin," she said.

"So now Oscar is a serial killer?" Edna took another drink of whisky. No matter how improbable, most of the evidence pointed to Oscar Winchester.

"How?" Horace asked.

"It could be arsenic poisoning via the herbal drink," said Frederick. "Marjorie almost drank some, but I stopped her."

"But wouldn't Jasmin be dead by now?" Edna asked.

"Not if it's administered in low doses, but there would be symptoms that could mimic any number of illnesses of old age."

"Blimey."

"Did Johnson find out anything more about the company finances?' Marjorie asked Frederick.

He shook his head. "No time."

"You said Johnson discovered two things," said Horace. "What was the second?"

"Nothing concrete, but the shouting he heard was a man and a woman arguing in the grounds. That's what drew him outside in the first place."

"Georgina and Oscar? Just like I said, case solved." Edna sat back triumphantly.

Marjorie was about to agree, but then thought about it. "Except, as we mentioned before Frederick arrived, if that were the case, someone else must have hit Johnson over the head."

"He couldn't swear to who he heard. There's more than one woman in the house," said Frederick. "It had gone quieter by the time he got near and he thinks everyone was back from wherever they had been this morning by then. Anyone could have coshed him."

"My money's on Jamie," said Horace.

"I'm inclined to agree, which points us back to a conspiracy to commit murder between Jamie Peeble and his boss." Marjorie saw Edna's face drop. "At least one of them is out of the way. Horace's right about one thing. If David Cribb suspects Jamie's involvement, he's in danger."

"Okay, so what's the plan?" Edna sat upright. Marjorie was pleased to see she had more colour to her face.

"Good to see you're going to help now rather than drink whisky," Marjorie said with a giggle. "You and Horace keep an eye on David and make sure nothing happens to him. Frederick and I will break the news to Jasmin."

"And while we're at it, we'll get a sample of that pick-me-up drink," added Frederick.

"More like a put-me-down if you're right," said Horace. "Should we tell David our suspicions?"

"I don't see why not. He'd have no reason to attack Georgina, and it's unlikely he's the poisoner. I'm sure everything is linked," Marjorie said. "By the way, would anyone like some strawberries?" She took the plastic container from her handbag.

Edna's eyes were on stalks. "Sometimes I think you're losing it, Marge."

Horace's brow had furrowed, as if he too thought she was losing her marbles.

Frederick smirked. "Johnson got the container to get a sample of the herbal drink," he explained, taking it and dropping the strawberries into a waste bin. He took out his own handkerchief and gave the container a thorough wipe. "That will have to do," he said. "I'm sure the lab can still get what they need."

Horace leapt up. "Right, team. Let's get to work. If we can get this crime solved by dinnertime, we might get to enjoy some more tennis tomorrow."

"Ain't you forgetting something, you lot?" Edna said. Marjorie raised a quizzical eyebrow. "What about involving the person who needs to know, DI Patricia Bloom?"

The excited flutter in Marjorie's heart slowed when she was faced with this challenge.

"Edna's right," said Frederick.

Marjorie sighed. "Let's get the sample from Jasmin's room first then we'll let the police know what's happening before anyone tries to stop us. David has a tendency to keep her out of things it's imperative she knows. Better to hear from us than the police that her son's been arrested on suspicion of murder and attempted murder."

"It could still turn out to be a double murder," said Horace. "I'm not sure Georgina will pull through."

"Either way, it's important Jasmin knows what's happening. Frederick and I will see the police afterwards. The inspector left about the same time as Oscar, so I expect she's interviewing him. I could phone her."

"Er--"

Frederick was interrupted. "You ain't her favourite person at the minute, so don't expect a warm reception if you do," Edna warned.

"Too bad."

Frederick managed to speak. "I've been trying to say, she's back and didn't seem in any hurry. I took a peep when I got back from the hospital in case you were beyond the cordon. I heard her telling someone Oscar had requested a solicitor who happened to be in court. She was watching everything the CSIs were doing."

Horace's eyes creased. "Just like last time," he said, laughing.

Marjorie remembered how thorough DI Bloom had been on the shores of Loch Ness when she herself had stumbled across a body. The other police officers thought she was too slow, but she was, in fact, meticulous.

"She'll be a few hours yet," Marjorie said with a chuckle.

"The inspector will want to do everything by the book before she interviews Oscar with some expensive solicitor present," said Horace.

"Let's get on, then. I bet Jamie's done a runner. I'm sure he's got a record, and not one of the musical variety." Horace snorted and Edna finally saw the funny side, which sent them both into shrieks of laughter. Frederick rolled his eyes. Marjorie refocussed, feeling a fire in her chest that wouldn't be extinguished until justice was served for Gordon, for Georgina and, if they were right, for Jasmin.

"Time to catch a killer," she said, giving Frederick a determined stare.

Chapter 28

Lady Marjorie Snellthorpe and Frederick Mackworth stood on the threshold of Jasmin Winchester's room. The afternoon sunlight was fading outside the window and the room was dull and quiet. Marjorie tapped on the open door before entering, then glanced around as they stepped inside, her eyes darting from the bed, where Jasmin sat propped up by pillows, to the bedside table and the jug of herbal remedy perched on it. As the sun came out from behind a cloud, Marjorie noticed Jasmin's skin had taken on a sallow hue. They had no proof that Oscar was to blame for the poisoning, or even if the poisoning was anything more than a theory, but they would find out soon enough.

Following the long afternoon nap, Jasmin's eyes looked much more alert than they had at lunchtime.

"Good afternoon, Jasmin," Marjorie said, trying to sound cheerful. "I hope you've had a pleasant rest."

Jasmin smiled weakly. "As good as can be expected with the curtains open."

Marjorie accepted the rebuke. She had not closed them when she left her friend earlier.

"I apologise. Your patio garden is so lovely, I didn't want to deprive you of the view."

"It is rather special," Jasmin agreed. She drew her legs over the side of the bed while Frederick averted his eyes. "I'll get my dressing gown from the bathroom, and then perhaps you will join me for tea."

"We'd like that," said Marjorie.

As soon as Jasmin left the room, Marjorie stepped forward, her gaze fixed firmly on the jug of herbal remedy. She stretched out her hand and picked it up, motioning for Frederick to keep an eye on the bathroom door before her other hand reached into her handbag for the plastic container. She poured a small amount of the liquid inside and replaced the seal just in time, placing the sample inside her handbag.

"Shall I make the tea?" asked Frederick.

"The kitchen's through there," said Marjorie, pointing to the room where she had been the previous morning.

Frederick was already on his way. "Yes. I noticed it when David was here the other night."

"Why are you looking so serious, Marjorie?" Jasmin asked.

"I'm afraid this is the second time in a few days I have to be the bearer of bad news," she said.

"That sounds ominous."

Marjorie didn't know where to begin. "This afternoon, your daughter-in-law… Georgina was…" she paused, searching for the right words. "Georgina has been… stabbed. She's alive, but it doesn't look good."

Jasmin gasped, her hand flying to her mouth. Her eyes welled up.

"Surely not Georgina," she whispered. "There must be some mistake."

"I'm afraid not. The police are still outside. They have made an arrest."

"Is it the same person who killed poor Gordon?"

"The police believe so. Jasmin, this isn't easy to tell you, but they believe Oscar is responsible for the crimes. They found him next to Georgina with a knife in his hand."

Jasmin's eyes widened in horror. She shook her head. "That can't be right," she said. "Oscar would never do anything like that. They have their problems, but he loves Georgina."

Marjorie and Frederick exchanged a glance, both of them aware of what others had said. Did Jasmin know about Georgina's affair or Oscar's infidelity? Could there be more to this sorry story? Marjorie was wondering whether she had misjudged Oscar and whether he might have been framed. What was it he had wanted to speak to her about?

If only he had joined us for dinner, like he'd promised.

She shook the scrambling thoughts away. All the evidence suggested Oscar was guilty. What she needed to discover was whether he was working alone.

Frederick brought tea through, and Marjorie and Jasmin sat in almost identical positions as they had previously. Frederick took a stool.

"Jasmin, I may have mentioned before that on the day I arrived, Oscar told me he wanted to speak to me. He was… well… mysterious. Do you have any idea what he might have wanted to say?" It was a long shot, but worth a try.

Taking her cup and saucer from Frederick, Jasmin furrowed her brow. "It could have been something to do with the business. Something isn't right, but I don't know what it is. Oscar and David have been plotting something. They think I don't notice, but they go silent whenever I walk into a room. Hugh left me this house and a controlling interest in the hotel chain, so they should keep me informed. Whenever I ask, Oscar says he doesn't like to worry me."

Marjorie's curiosity was piqued. "What does your interest mean in day-to-day terms?"

"For the most part, nothing. Oscar takes overall responsibility and David does what he's always done... offers a guiding hand. But when it comes to any major changes, stock sales or new acquisitions, I have to give my approval. David helps me to decide."

Frederick eyed Marjorie to press further. She hated the intrusion, but asked, "Has any of this led to friction between you and Oscar, or David and Oscar?"

"Not that I've noticed, but as I say, something has been brewing. Perhaps that's what Oscar wanted to speak to you about, Marjorie." She smiled grimly. "This is mere supposition because I don't know. Oscar could have been wanting to get you on his side to help convince me of a business move, especially if David is opposed to whatever it is he might be planning. But this is irrelevant while my son is suspected of murder. Marjorie, I'm begging you... find out who killed Gordon and who is responsible for attacking Georgina, because it wasn't my son."

Marjorie sipped her tea, deep in thought, before looking up at Jasmin. "If Oscar is innocent, we will prove it."

"And where's David?" Jasmin asked. "Does he know what's happened? He'll make everything all right." The signs that Jasmin was losing focus crossed her face again.

Marjorie hadn't realised just how much power David Cribb held in this household. Alarm bells sounded in her head.

"David knows about Oscar's arrest. He's trying to find Jamie at present to see what he knows. Would you like us to ask him to come to you?"

Jasmin shook her head, tears falling down her cheeks. "I need some time alone, if you don't mind? People can't see me like this. I'll take a shower and get dressed. I need to sort out the dinner arrangements and I must speak to the police."

"You don't need to worry about any of that for now," said Frederick.

Marjorie stood. "We should go now and let you get ready," she said, placing a comforting hand on Jasmin's shoulder. "We'll let David know you'll be up soon to arrange things for the evening." Marjorie felt a sense of purpose might help Jasmin. She already looked stronger for it.

"Please find out who is responsible for these terrible crimes, Marjorie." Jasmin's eyes pleaded once more, her face still a mask of shock. Marjorie understood what a mother would do for an only son, no matter how much they might differ.

As Marjorie and Frederick left the bedroom, her mind was racing.

"We must get this sample to DI Bloom. It's time to tell her all we know before anyone else sees us."

"I've just had a thought," said Frederick. "When we tell the inspector our suspicions, she could take the whole jug from the bedroom."

"I agree, but just in case the poisoner is someone other than Oscar and they try to do a switch," Marjorie tapped her handbag, "this is our backup."

"Do you think David is less of a suitor and more of a predator after hearing about his influence?"

"The thought has crossed my mind," said Marjorie, hoping she was wrong. "If it's the latter, I'm not sure Jasmin will be able to take much more. We have to tread with extreme caution."

"We'd better hurry and speak to DI Bloom. If Horace tells David about our poison suspicions and he's involved, who knows what he'll do?"

Frederick was right. They hurried towards the front door. It was imperative they find out if Oscar had killed Georgina and whether he'd had help from Jamie, or whether the killer was someone else who had been orchestrating everything while hatching a devilish plan to implicate Oscar. The thought of someone getting away with murder sent shockwaves running through Marjorie's spine.

Chapter 29

DI Bloom was on her way into the house when Marjorie and Frederick reached the front door.

"I want to speak to your friends before I leave," she said, all pretence at friendliness having evaporated.

"And we need to speak to you, Inspector." Marjorie stood her ground. Patricia Bloom stopped in her tracks; intense eyes fixed on Marjorie's as if weighing up whether she had the time to waste.

"What is it?"

"I'm sorry we didn't mention the affair before. That was my fault, but we didn't feel it was relevant at the time."

"And now a woman is fighting for her life," Bloom snapped, eyes blazing. "If she dies, is that on you too, Lady Marjorie?"

Marjorie winced.

"That's not fair," snapped Frederick.

DI Bloom let out a heavy sigh and Marjorie noticed the dark shadows around her eyes. "You're right. I'm sorry. It's been a long couple of days."

"If Georgina dies, Inspector, believe me when I tell you it will be a lifelong regret…" There was no time to spare. Marjorie saw David Cribb heading their way out of the corner of her eye. "But I can't stress enough how important it is that you listen to me now."

"Inspector, I have to speak to you." David glared at Marjorie. "These people…" he waved his arms at her and Frederick "…believe Jasmin Winchester is being slowly poisoned. It appears Oscar may be responsible for that too."

Brilliant manoeuvre, thought Marjorie.

"Is this true?" DI Bloom looked at Marjorie.

"Frederick suspects someone has been poisoning Mrs Winchester with arsenic, that much is right, but as to the who by—"

DI Bloom's head shot in Frederick's direction. "You were a pharmacist, weren't you?"

"Yes," said Frederick, flushing. "I'm surprised you remembered."

"Medium?" Bloom snapped.

"A herbal drink. You'll find a jug on Mrs Winchester's bedside table."

"Blaby!" DI Bloom bellowed to her sergeant unnecessarily as he was standing next to her. "Retrieve the jug from Mrs Winchester's bedside and take it out to Brenda. Tell her it needs testing for arsenic and any other poison."

"Please don't mention poisoning to Jasmin," Marjorie said.

"I agree on that point, Inspector. Mrs Winchester has been through enough over the past few days." David shot Marjorie another steely glare.

"Hear that, Blaby? Be discreet."

"Yes, Ma'am."

"Is Brenda the pathologist, Brenda Stamp?" Frederick asked.

DI Bloom's eyes widened. "Yes, do you know her?"

Frederick shook his head. "I don't, but I've seen her at work." He grinned, recalling observing the pathologist putting another DI in his place during the Christmas investigation.

"Well, if you'll all excuse me, I need to interview Mr Tyler and Mrs Parkinton." Horace and Edna had caught up with the entourage by this point. "I take it we can use Oscar Winchester's sitting room again?"

"Of course, Inspector. I'll come with you to make sure it's empty. There's something else I need to mention anyway."

Marjorie sighed. David Cribb had derailed her mission and now he was no doubt going to feed the inspector with more ammunition against Oscar.

"I thought you'd be pleased," said Horace, hanging back.

"It seems we may have been too quick to clear him. We don't know whether David is friend or foe at the moment. Try to listen in to what he tells DI Bloom."

"Will do," Horace said, chasing after the pack.

"And would you see if you can send Edna back?" called Marjorie after his retreating figure. "I need a word with her before you go through."

"Righto," he replied over his shoulder.

Marjorie and Frederick watched the DI and her gaggle follow David to Oscar's sitting room. A few minutes later, Edna returned and Marjorie took her to one side while Frederick made sure no-one was in earshot.

"Do you think you could make your excuses to get away for a little while?"

"I guess so, Marge, but what for?"

"Knowing how good you are at searching guest bedrooms, I'd like you to check a few while Frederick and I do some research down here."

"I don't know, Marge. What if I'm found?"

"You'll think of something."

"Okay, whose rooms and how do I find them?"

"As many as you can, but definitely Terry's, Jamie's and, if you have time, Paris's."

"Not Oscar's?"

"Too risky. The police might be doing that as we speak. If you call Johnson, I'm sure he'll know which room is Jamie's, and Terry and Paris's rooms are in the same corridor as ours."

"No promises, but I'll see what I can do. Remember, they might be locked."

"In which case, find the master keys. I keep mine hanging in my hall," said Marjorie.

DC Sudhik appeared at their side and cleared his throat. "Erm, excuse me, but the DI wants to speak to Mrs Parkinton now."

"See you later, Marge," Edna said before following the DC to Oscar's sitting room.

Sergeant Blaby gave them a nod when he passed them on his way out with the jug.

"What was that all about?" Frederick asked.

"Just a hunch," said Marjorie. "It might be nothing."

"David's clever, isn't he?" said Frederick. "Instead of trying to conceal the evidence, he's delivered it to them on a platter."

"Hmm, I'm not sure yet if he's clever, stupid or innocent," Marjorie said.

"She's wrong, you know… implying you, or any of us, are responsible for the attack on Georgina Winchester."

"I sincerely hope so."

"Marjorie, the only person responsible for that is the one who stabbed her. Even if the police had known about the affair earlier, they wouldn't have had enough evidence to arrest Oscar. He'd have invented an alibi, most likely with the backup of Jamie."

Marjorie pursed her lips. "I'm not so sure about that. We're being taken for interfering fools. I believe someone has been using my relationship with Hugh and Jasmin to weave a murderous plan, and I'm becoming less and less convinced of Oscar's guilt. He – and therefore, we – are pawns in someone else's masterplan."

"David Cribb's?" Frederick said.

"That's what we need to find out. Do you know whether he has an office on this floor?"

"He does." Vic had appeared from nowhere.

"How much did you overhear?" Marjorie asked.

"Enough," he said. "We might only work here, Lady Marjorie, but we care about Mrs Winchester senior and like Mrs Winchester junior. If you think someone other than Oscar has been trying to do either of them harm, then John and I will help in any way we can."

"Thank you. In that case, please lead the way," said Marjorie. "When one door closes, another opens," she whispered to Frederick.

Vic led them to a wing of the house where they hadn't ventured before. "These are private rooms used by Oscar mostly, but David has an office along here." He stopped dead at a door and tried the handle. It was locked.

"Now what?" Frederick asked.

Vic winked, reaching into his pocket for a bunch of keys. "Jamie keeps these in his room downstairs, but as he seems to have disappeared, I took the liberty." It didn't take long for Vic to find the right key and open the door for them. "I'd better not stay just in case. I don't want to lose my job."

"You've been most helpful, Vic. Thank you," said Marjorie.

"If I see David, I'll try to keep him away from this area. More than likely he'll be with Mrs Winchester and the others and, if he is, I want to be around to hear what goes on." Vic's face set hard.

"I wouldn't want to get on the wrong side of him," said Frederick after Vic had left and they'd entered the office.

"No, but an excellent ally. The men in white have turned out to be cavalry rather than the menaces we took them for."

Marjorie surveyed the office, her eyes adjusting to the dim light in this part of the house. A sizeable mahogany desk with a brown leather chair pushed underneath was situated under the large window. Old-fashioned lace netting over the window made the room darker than necessary. A bookshelf housing folders stood against the wall with a filing cabinet next to it.

"What are we looking for?" Frederick asked, taking the seat behind the desk.

"Anything that points to why David might want Jasmin out of the way, or that proves his innocence."

Frederick began rifling through papers on the desk while Marjorie headed straight to the filing cabinet. The key was in place, so she unlocked it and pulled open the top drawer. It was filled with a plethora of folders. Each one was labelled, most relating to dates long past. There was a mountain of delivery notes, minutes of meetings and purchase orders from when Hugh Winchester was still alive.

Marjorie bypassed these and tried the next drawer down. The indexes were more recent. She pulled a folder from a pocket labelled Miscellaneous Business. This one was at the back and had the most recent date. She opened it. Inside were documents relating to the extraneous use of Oscar's hotels.

Her eyes scanned the papers, taking in the enormity of what she had found. "Look at these," she said to Frederick.

Frederick rose from the desk and took the papers she handed to him. "What's he up to?"

Marjorie frowned. "It appears someone has been using Oscar's hotels to set up shady deals, not to mention a few becoming high-class brothels."

"There's enough here to convince the inspector she should look elsewhere," Frederick said quietly, flipping through the file. "They've also been taking money from Jasmin."

Marjorie gasped in shock as her mind raced with questions. How long had this been going on? Who else was involved? What would happen if Jasmin found out? As she continued reading through the files, she began piecing together a bigger picture.

"Just a minute. Look."

Frederick read the document she held in her hand. It contained details of money from the hotels and Jasmin's account being funnelled into concealed accounts. There had also been fake companies set up to launder money. It appeared David had been involved in this for quite some time.

Frederick handed her a final document. "I found this in the top drawer of his desk." It was Jasmin's will. Marjorie read through it and glanced at Frederick.

"And now we know why it is necessary to get Jasmin out of the way. It's time to see Inspector Bloom."

Chapter 30

"I don't know what else to say, Inspector. As far as we're aware, Oscar was not carrying a knife when he left the house." Horace reiterated what he had been telling DI Bloom for the past twenty minutes.

"But you agree he could have picked one up on his way out," she said.

This conversation was going round in circles, as far as Edna could see. She could understand Inspector Bloom being disappointed that they couldn't give her a picture of Oscar dashing out of the house, dagger in hand, but they were telling the truth.

Suddenly, the door burst open and Jasmin Winchester entered, accompanied by Terry, Paris and David.

"I must speak with you about my son, Inspector Bloom," Jasmin said. "I've brought Terry and Paris along to back up what I have to say."

Brilliant! It couldn't have played better into Edna's hands. "If you'll excuse me, I've had a terrible shock this afternoon and I'm still feeling queasy. Do you mind if Horace and I leave you to it?"

DI Bloom didn't seem happy about the intrusion, but took one look at the determined Jasmin and waved a hand, sighing.

"Fine," she huffed.

Once they were out of the room, Edna grabbed Horace's arm. "We've got work to do."

"So much for you feeling queasy," Horace replied, grinning.

"It worked, didn't it?" She put a finger to her lips while they passed members of the CSI team working around a sheath hanging on the wall.

"That must be where Oscar, or whoever, got the dagger," said Horace once they were a safe distance away.

Edna didn't like to think about the knife because it brought back the horrific image of the pallid Georgina Winchester lying on the ground.

"This way," she said, moving towards the front door. There, she mooched around the coat hooks and stands.

"What are you looking for?" Horace asked.

Edna blew out a breath. There was nothing there.

"Let's try downstairs," she said, marching off.

Once they got near the kitchen, she noticed a row of uniforms and staff coats hanging in the small hallway leading to the scullery. The latter was still cordoned off.

"I can't help if you don't tell me what we're looking for," Horace complained.

Edna reached a hand up and grabbed a set of keys. "These," she said, triumphant.

Horace's eyes registered what she had in her hand. "This is what Marjorie wanted to speak to you about," he said.

"Yeah. Come on. We've got rooms to search while that lot is busy."

Horace seemed happy to follow. "This reminds me of Christmas," he said.

"Except Marge wasn't happy about us rooting in her guests' rooms, but she's more than happy for us to check them out here."

When they got up to the first floor, they saw two rooms at the end of the corridor on which they were staying with police tape outside.

"They must be Oscar and Georgina's, Marge said to leave them. We need to find Terry Kemble's, Paris's and Jamie's," Edna explained.

"What about David's?"

"I think he's got a suite on the ground floor somewhere – too risky."

Horace rubbed his forehead. "There are a lot of rooms along here, Edna. This could take all day."

"You're right. We need help."

"Are you looking for someone?" John appeared behind them, eyeing the bunch of keys in Edna's hand.

"Erm…"

"Don't worry, Vic just let your Lady Marjorie and her friend into David's office downstairs. We're happy to help as long as it's going to help Mrs Winchester Senior."

"In which case, could you tell us where we can find some rooms? Terry's, Paris's and Jamie's?" Horace said.

John raised a thick eyebrow at the mention of the third name. "You can forget about Jamie. He's packed a bag and gone."

Horace and Edna exchanged a glance. "Sounds like he's afraid of something," Edna said.

"Or maybe he's decided he doesn't want to work for a would-be murderer. He hates the job anyway."

"Okay. So what about the others?" Edna said.

John lumbered along the corridor. He stopped about four doors down from Frederick's room.

"That's Terry's. Paris's is back that way, three doors before yours." He looked at Horace.

"Thanks," said Horace.

"See you put them back when you're done." John pointed to the keys Edna was gripping tightly before he turned around and headed back towards the spiral staircase.

"That was lucky. Good thing Marge got them onside," Edna said.

Horace tried the door. "Locked," he said. "You'd better give me those."

"Why? Because you're a man?"

"No, because your hands are shaking," said Horace.

He was right. Adrenaline was rushing through Edna's body, making her tremble. With that and the exertion of climbing the stairs bringing on the unwelcome breathlessness, she capitulated, handing the keys over. Edna resolved to get herself checked out when she got home, just in case the cancer was coming back. Either way, she would have to consider getting a stairlift installed or moving to a bungalow in the near future.

Horace was already in Terry's room before Edna brought herself back to the present. "Get a grip!" she told herself and hurried inside, closing the door behind her in case the police or CSIs decided now was the time to search Oscar and Georgina's rooms.

There was nothing to be found in Terry's room other than designer clothes, bags and shoes. "He's got more clothes in this wardrobe than I've owned my entire life," said Horace.

Edna picked up a Rolex off the bedside table. "Blimey! How many of these has he got? He doesn't even live here."

Apart from confirmation that Terry Kemble liked expensive brands and luxury goods, there was nothing incriminating. "It makes you wonder if Paris's assumption that he's embezzling funds is right."

"I wouldn't take anything that woman says as gospel. She's as sour as vinegar, that one. He runs a hotel chain. I expect he earns a lot of money and as far as I've seen, there's no wife, so why not spend it while you can if that's what you want to do?"

Horace chuckled away. "Sour as vinegar. I've not heard that one before."

"Good, you don't know everything, then, ain't it? Come on. There's nothing to find in here. Speaking of sour, let's go to Paris Toliver's room."

Chapter 31

Nobody noticed when Marjorie and Frederick entered Oscar's sitting room. The unruly crowd was too busy speaking over each other. Marjorie was pleased to see almost everyone was there. Horace and Edna came in soon afterwards and Edna gave Marjorie a nod.

DI Bloom was on the phone standing by the window, which in part explained the chaotic scene. Once she got off the phone, the inspector motioned for people to be quiet.

"You'll be pleased to hear that Georgina Winchester has just come out of surgery and is out of danger. The surgeon stemmed the bleeding. She's received a few litres of blood and we'll be able to interview her in the morning."

Marjorie scanned the faces around her. "Not everyone will be pleased to hear the news." A hush filled the room as every head spun in her direction.

Paris rounded on Marjorie. "What are you talking about? Of course we're pleased."

"We'll see about that," said Marjorie, undeterred. "I have in my hand a file, the contents of which will go a long way to explaining some, if not all, of what's been happening, even before my friends and I arrived. Might I suggest we all sit down?"

The stunned occupants did as she said. Terry Kemble looked miserable as he rubbed a scratch to his neck extending from his designer collar, which showed spots of blood. Vic and John stood on the fringes with determined expressions on their faces. David Cribb sat next to Jasmin, looking nonplussed.

DI Bloom took the file from Marjorie and quickly leafed through it. After reading the file, Bloom barked for DC Sudhik to stand at the door.

"Over to you, Lady Marjorie." DI Bloom was gracious enough to accept the contents of the file required clarification, although Marjorie herself didn't have all the answers. She hoped Horace and Edna could fill in the gaps.

Satisfied Vic and John would help the police if trouble broke out, Marjorie moved over to the fireplace and began.

"I must admit I was bemused when Oscar Winchester contacted me out of the blue, asking to speak to my late husband, and even more so when he invited my friends and me to spend this week here."

"You would always be welcome in my home, Marjorie," said Jasmin.

"But you weren't told we were coming until the last minute, Jasmin. Only Oscar knew. Another person soon discovered that if they didn't act fast, it wouldn't be long before they were exposed." Marjorie noticed a few quizzical raised eyebrows and heard an audible gasp from Jasmin. "With Oscar growing suspicious of dubious dealings going on behind his back, I had to ask myself why he didn't go to the person he would trust the most: his father's lifelong friend and adviser, David Cribb?"

Marjorie glowered at David who shook his head, palms uppermost. He looked as though he had been struck when Jasmin pulled her hand away from his.

"Good point, Marge," said Edna, giving David her own visual dagger.

"Quite simply, it was because he no longer trusted his father's oldest friend. Oscar was so desperate for outside help, he phoned another of his father's close friends. One he knew to be beyond reproach: my husband, Ralph Snellthorpe. His reaction on hearing that my husband was no longer alive was touching, but extraordinary. He sounded far more devastated than one would expect from someone who barely knew Ralph when I broke the news.

"This was something I found odd at the time and, in many ways, it should have alerted me that something was amiss. But in the end, it was that genuine reaction that caused me to accept his invitation when he called back a few days later – he was most insistent we come." Marjorie looked apologetically towards her friends.

"Oscar made it clear on the day we arrived that he wanted to speak to me about something, asking me to keep it secret, even from his mother. He appeared troubled. Alas, other events had also occurred before we arrived on that day. Oscar had discovered his wife was having an affair with Gordon Collins and, not long before that, he had succumbed to pressure to add an extra beneficiary to his mother's will."

Frederick held aloft the will in his hand.

Jasmin's jaw dropped. "Oscar only told me it needed updating he didn't mention any beneficiary changes to the document. I signed it without a thought."

"But what Oscar didn't know was that this new beneficiary was impatient about your longevity and was resorting to slowly poisoning you, Jasmin. Although Oscar had suspicions about your declining health, which is why he was being overprotective."

Vic stared at David Cribb with one of those looks that might be enough to kill, if a look wielded such power.

Marjorie went on. "No doubt the poisoner had contrived to convince Oscar that you, Jasmin, were soon to be leaving this earth for natural reasons. I'm sure that will come to light when the inspector asks him."

Jasmin turned to David, blinking back tears. "You?"

"No. Not David," Edna cut in. "This scheme is all down to Paris Toliver. She has convinced your son she is his father's secret love child and threatened to tell you if Oscar didn't pay her a large sum of money and add her to the will."

Edna's foraging had been successful; Marjorie was delighted. She continued, "It must have been when Oscar withdrew a large sum of money to pay Paris that he realised something was amiss with the hotels."

"This is ridiculous. I'm not staying here and listening to this nonsense. So what if I asked for a share in my father's inheritance and for a loan? My business was struggling. It's only right my half-family helps." Paris jumped up, trying to leave, but Vic blocked her way.

"Except you're no more Hugh Winchester's daughter than I am," said Edna. "Here's the fictional birth certificate, along with the fictional DNA result." She handed two pieces of paper to DI Bloom, "And here's a copy of the real one I photographed. Amazing what you can find on these family tree websites." Edna handed her phone to the inspector.

Paris folded her arms, pouting. "Okay, so I tried to pull a fast one. This family's rich enough and I am a good friend. Oscar's always treated me like a dogsbody."

"That don't make you entitled to what ain't yours," said Edna.

Marjorie hadn't known why Paris had been added to the will so recently, but she had suspected it might be something to do with blackmail. This was closer to home for Edna than Marjorie had imagined, but her cousin-in-law was a fierce advocate when required.

"It still doesn't mean I tried to poison anyone."

Edna harrumphed, pulling yet another document from her handbag. Marjorie wondered what that might contain.

"Except your boyfriend, Dr Mitchell Prior – Dr Mitchell Liar, more like – isn't a specialist from Harley Street. He's a fraud, a mere homeopath with no qualifications whatsoever. Here, Inspector, is a copy of the medical report he made out after examining Jasmin, pretending she had a terminal illness and recommending a herbal remedy as a tonic."

Jasmin's mouth was wide open. "Dr Prior isn't a doctor?"

"Nope," said Edna, clearly enjoying herself. "He even charged Oscar eight hundred pounds for the consultation. More than he earns in a week, most likely."

"I think we've got enough to go on for now," said DI Bloom. "I'm sure we'll find more evidence following a police search." She gave Edna and Horace a disapproving stare before turning to Marjorie. "Are you suggesting that Miss Toliver also killed Gordon Collins and attacked Georgina Winchester?"

"I DID NOT!" Paris got up, almost hysterical, but Vic gave her a rough shove back to her seat.

The last threads were falling into place for Marjorie. "No, Inspector. Although it is she who inadvertently set in motion the sequence of events leading to both attacks. What I believe happened – and those documents confirm it – is that Oscar asked Gordon to look into what was going on in the business. It also explains why he was so angry at finding out that the accountant he had put his trust in was having an affair with his wife. When he asked Gordon to investigate, Oscar didn't know who else he could trust, and that's when he called me, or rather, Ralph.

"Despite the affair, Gordon was good at his job, uncovering details of corruption within the hotels alongside other dubious dealings. That's what he came to tell Oscar about on the night he was murdered."

DI Bloom shuffled through the papers in her hand. "So, it's this man, then?" She showed Marjorie a sheet.

"What is that file and where did you get it?" Jasmin asked.

"From David Cribb's office. It was in his filing cabinet," said Frederick.

David's head shot up. "What is this? Surely you can't think I had anything to do with any of this? I've never seen that folder before in my life."

Jasmin looked distraught.

"I believe you," said Marjorie. "When we entered the room, I admit we thought you were the most likely perpetrator, but the whole time the inspector has held that folder in her hand, I've been observing you for a reaction and there wasn't one."

Marjorie looked at DI Bloom. "Whoever killed Gordon took these files from his briefcase and placed them in David's filing cabinet to incriminate him if framing Oscar didn't work. On reflection, the page suggesting David's involvement doesn't match the others. I'm sure your experts will confirm that, Inspector. Had you charged Oscar, these documents would have been unnecessary and would have miraculously disappeared."

"So who killed Gordon?" Jasmin asked.

"And tried to kill Georgina? Was it Jamie?" David added.

"I'm afraid the killer is Terry Kemble," said Marjorie. "Not satisfied with embezzling funds from the European hotels, he has set up false businesses in the UK, diverting funds from Oscar's legitimate business and some of Jasmin's personal money in the process."

"That's a lie! You have no proof," Terry yelled.

"He's right. There's nothing here implicating him," said DI Bloom.

"No, he's not that stupid. He removed everything naming him, but what he doesn't know is that, on the night he died, Gordon searched his room." Marjorie looked hopefully at Edna, but she shook her head. Disappointed that her theory might not be enough, Marjorie had an idea.

"I believe Gordon photographed evidence on his phone. Later that night, Terry lured Gordon into a meeting he thought would be with him and Oscar, perhaps saying he would explain everything to both of them. Gordon would have hidden his phone upon realising he had been set up. I suspect it will be close to where he died."

"Forensics searched the area," Terry sneered, looking more confident. Marjorie feared he would have covered his tracks well since killing Gordon, which is why he had been so desperate to get out of the house the morning after the murder. Where could it be?

"We have Gordon's phone. There was nothing like that on it," said DI Bloom.

Marjorie felt the truth was getting away from her until help came from an unlikely source.

Paris said, "Gordon had two phones. The other night when he marched in and had a barney with Terry, he showed him something on his phone, but later on, when he tried to call Oscar, Gordon took another one from a different pocket."

Marjorie slapped her head. "Of course! One for wife and work, and one for his lover. Alison, the house manager, interrupted him when he was searching Terry's room the other night. In his haste, not wanting to be caught again, he must have used the wrong phone to take the pictures. Knowing he would be meeting with Oscar, he hid that one to be on the safe side. At that time, he was no doubt going down to the kitchen, as he often did, to make himself a drink while waiting for Oscar to come home. Not realising his killer knew his habits and was lying in wait, probably outside the back door, until he heard Oscar's car coming up the driveway and then he pounced."

Terry Kemble remained arrogant and cocksure. "Prove it," he said.

Marjorie had a sudden thought. "Did you check the housekeepers' uniforms? They're hanging up at the bottom of the stairs near to the scullery. Gordon could have slipped a phone into one of them, meaning to collect it after his meeting with Terry and Oscar."

DI Bloom waved a hand at DC Sudhik, who left the room. John took his place in front of the door.

"Can't you see this woman's senile? She'll make you the laughingstock of Scotland Yard," Terry yelled.

DI Bloom answered, "This woman, as you call her, is incredible. Please could I have your car keys, Mr Kemble?"

Kemble rubbed his scratched neck. "What for? Why should I?"

"It would be better if you cooperate, sir." DI Bloom stared him down. Reluctantly, he took a key card from his pocket and handed it over.

"Blaby, arrest Mr Kemble and read him his rights. We'll pull all the pieces together later. In the meantime, ask the CSI manager to search his car, see if they can match the rope fibres."

Terry Kemble's face turned crimson. DS Blaby did as instructed while Terry made a less confident protestation of his innocence.

"That scratch on your neck. I assume it came from a black cat called Ben?" Marjorie said.

Kemble scowled at her. "Stupid animal. It could be rabid. They should put it down."

"On the contrary, the intelligent creature was the only witness to your devious deed."

DI Bloom's forehead scrunched.

Marjorie chuckled. "Ben, the black cat, was in the scullery on the night Gordon was murdered. He saw the whole thing. Cats never forget. I expect if Mr Kemble hasn't already had his suit dry cleaned, your team will find cat hair too."

DI Bloom summoned the uniformed officers from the front door to take a ranting Terry away.

"And don't forget Miss Toliver," she said to Blaby.

"I won't, Ma'am."

Everyone else remained in Oscar's sitting room, waiting for the shouting of Terry Kemble to disappear into the distance. Paris was led away in a more dignified manner.

Chapter 32

Marjorie took the seat Paris had vacated, feeling drained.

"I take it the brothel side of the business is down to the bodyguard?" DI Bloom grinned, also taking a seat while holding up another piece of paper.

"It appears most of the people in Oscar's life were using him for something," Marjorie replied. "Whether that's because he's the way he is, or the other way around, who knows?"

"We can't find Jamie. He seems to have packed a bag and done a bunk," said David.

"He won't get far," said DI Bloom.

"Terry Kemble also assaulted my chauffer, Inspector, but I'm not sure we'll be able to prove it."

"Why don't I know about this?"

"We found Johnson while you were in the throes of arresting Oscar. Before Georgina was attacked, I think Johnson overheard Oscar arguing with his wife, and Terry saw an opportunity to make doubly sure of framing Oscar. He hit Johnson over the head, most probably after watching the couple storming off in opposite directions. Seeing where Georgina was headed, he nipped into the house for a dagger and took his opportunity."

"Making it look like Oscar had done the deed and thinking Johnson would testify to them having had an argument," said Frederick.

"Something like that. He's a ruthless opportunist who sought to improve his chances of framing Oscar for murder by stabbing an innocent woman. No doubt he knew Oscar would turn around and try to make amends with his wife. In doing so, Oscar was found at the scene of the crime."

"So David did nothing wrong?" Jasmin asked.

"Nothing at all, but the men in your life could let you breathe and be less overprotective," said Edna, giving David a warning look.

David held his palms up. "I will. I promise."

Edna smirked. "Looks like we did it again, Marge," she said, but no-one was looking at her.

David was shifting nervously from the settee. He got down on one knee, taking a ring from his pocket.

"I've lacked the courage to do this before, but I don't want to waste any more time. If you'll have me, Jasmin, I'd like to marry you."

"Oh, David," said Jasmin.

"Is that a yes?" he asked.

"Of course it's a yes." Jasmin's eyes brightened.

"I bet that's not something you see every day, Inspector," said Edna, nudging DI Bloom, whose face flushed.

"Just a minute. I'm forgetting something. Is Oscar also innocent?" Jasmin turned to Marjorie, eyes sparkling.

"Totally," said Marjorie. "I'm sure he'll be released later."

DI Bloom nodded. "We'll take a statement, confirming his dealings with Gordon Collins as soon as I get back to the nick. I expect he'll corroborate what Lady Marjorie has told us."

"I don't know how to thank you," Jasmin said.

"No need. And it's not just me. We're a team," said Marjorie, smiling happily at her friends.

"Although Marge is chief investigator of the *awesome foursome*," said Edna, taking Marjorie's arm.

While they were enjoying the light aftermath of the arrests, DC Sudhik reappeared, waving a phone in his hand.

"Got it, Ma'am."

DI Bloom shook her head. "Uncanny, Lady Marjorie. If only I could recruit you into the Major Investigations Team."

Marjorie laughed. "Thank you, Inspector, but after a celebratory dinner and glass of champagne with the newly engaged couple, my friends and I are going to get a good night's sleep and enjoy the ladies' semi-finals day at Wimbledon tomorrow."

THE END

Author's Note

Thank you for reading *Murder at a Wimbledon Mansion*, the fourth full novel in the Lady Marjorie Snellthorpe series. If you have enjoyed it, please leave an honest review on any platform you may use.

If you would like to read the prequel to the series, the novella *Death of a Blogger* is available for free when you sign up for my newsletter, where you will receive news and offers once a month. If you prefer not to subscribe to newsletters, the book is available to purchase from most eBook stores, or to borrow, on request, from libraries. Print and audiobook versions are also available.

To find out what happens to our feisty pensioners next, keep an eye on my website at:
www.dawnbrookespublishing.com.

Discover where the Lady Marjorie character began; check out the Rachel Prince Mystery series.

Books by Dawn Brookes

Lady Marjorie Snellthorpe Mysteries

Death of a Blogger (prequel novella)
Murder at the Opera House
Murder in the Highlands
Murder at the Christmas Market
Murder at a Wimbledon Mansion
Murder in a Care Home (Coming soon)

Rachel Prince Mysteries

A Cruise to Murder
Deadly Cruise
Killer Cruise
Dying to Cruise
A Christmas Cruise Murder
Murderous Cruise Habit
Honeymoon Cruise Murder
A Murder Mystery Cruise
Hazardous Cruise
Captain's Dinner Cruise Murder
Corporate Cruise Murder
Treacherous Cruise Flirtation

Carlos Jacobi PI

Body in the Woods

The Bradgate Park Murders

The Museum Murders (coming soon)

Memoirs

Hurry up Nurse: Memoirs of nurse training in the 1970s

Hurry up Nurse 2: London calling

Hurry up Nurse 3: More adventures in the life of a student nurse

Picture Books for Children

Ava & Oliver's Bonfire Night Adventure
Ava & Oliver's Christmas Nativity Adventure
Danny the Caterpillar
Gerry the One-Eared Cat
Suki Seal and the Plastic Ring

Keep in touch:

Sign up for my no-spam newsletter at:
www.dawnbrookespublishing.com

Follow me on Facebook:
www.facebook.com/dawnbrookespublishing/

Follow me on TikTok
tiktok.com/@dawnbrookesauthor

Follow me on YouTube:
www.youtube.com/c/DawnBrookesPublishing

Acknowledgements

Thank you to my scrutiny team for the suggestions and amendments, making the finished version a more polished read. A particular thank you to the ex DCI on my advance team who advised on police procedure following a hanging.

Thanks to my editor Alison Jack for her fine-tuning and editing skills and to Alex Davis for proofreading the final document.

Thanks to my immediate circle of friends who are so patient with me when I'm absorbed in my fictional world for your continued support in all my endeavours.

Thank you so much to my Advance Reader Team for comments and support.

About the Author

Award-winning author Dawn Brookes is creator of the Rachel Prince Mystery series, combining a unique blend of murder, cruising and medicine with a touch of romance. She is also author of the Carlos Jacobi crime series and the Lady Marjorie Snellthorpe Mystery series.

Dawn holds an MA in Creative Writing with Distinction and has a 39-year nursing pedigree. She loves to travel and takes regular cruise holidays, which she says are for research purposes! She brings these passions and a love of clean crime to her writing.

The surname of her Rachel Prince protagonist is in honour of her childhood dog, Prince, who used to put his head on her knee while she lost herself in books.

Author of *Hurry up Nurse: memoirs of nurse training in the 1970s* and *Hurry up Nurse 2: London calling*, Dawn worked as a hospital nurse, midwife, district nurse and community matron across her career. Before turning her hand to writing for a living, she had multiple articles published in professional journals and coedited a nursing textbook.

She grew up in Leicester, later moved to London and Berkshire, but now lives in Derbyshire. Dawn holds a Bachelor's degree with Honours and a Master's degree in education. Writing across genres, she also writes for children. Dawn has a passion for nature and loves animals, especially dogs. Animals will continue to feature in her children's books, as she believes caring for animals and nature helps children to become kinder human beings.

Printed in Great Britain
by Amazon

43287121R00179